His faded jeans, worn boots, leather chaps and spurs were the fashion of the old West. He looked as rugged as the Texas hill country, and Tamara hoped he was here for a job.

He walked into the field with a slow-as-molasses swagger. "Ma'am," he said, his Texas drawl as thick as his mustache.

"Saw your ad." His mouth quirked. "Thought I could help out."

A sigh escaped her, and she told herself it was because of the possibility of hiring help, not from watching his lips move. "I tell you what," she said, "if you can start this tractor, you have the job."

He climbed aboard as if mounting a horse. He worked the gears, tried the ignition and the tractor came to life. A hint of a smile pulled at his mouth as he faced her.

"Well, I guess this means I've got the job."

Dear Reader,

The month of June makes me think of June brides, Father's Day and the first bloom of summer love. And Silhouette Romance is celebrating the start of summer with six wonderful books about love and romance.

Our BUNDLE OF JOY this month is delivered by Stella Bagwell's *The Tycoon's Tots*—her thirtieth Silhouette book. As her TWINS ON THE DOORSTEP miniseries continues, we finally discover who gets to keep those adorable babies...*and* find romance in the bargain.

Elizabeth August is back with her much-loved SMYTHESHIRE, MASSACHUSETTS series. In *The Determined Virgin* you'll meet a woman whose marriage of convenience is proving to be very *in*convenient, thanks to her intense attraction to her "in-name-only" husband.

BACHELOR GULCH is a little town that needs women, *and* the name of Sandra Steffen's brand-new miniseries. The fun begins in *Luke's Would-Be Bride* as a local bachelor falls for his feisty receptionist—the one woman in town *not* looking for a husband!

And there are plenty more compelling romances for you this month: A lovely lady rancher can't wait to hightail it out of Texas—till she meets her handsome new foreman in Leanna Wilson's *Lone Star Rancher*. A new husband can't bear to tell his amnesiac bride that the baby she's carrying isn't his, in *Her Forgotten Husband* by Anne Ha. And one lucky cowboy discovers a night of passion has just made him a daddy in Teresa Southwick's *The Bachelor's Baby*.

I hope you enjoy all of June's books!

Melissa Senate,
Senior Editor

Silhouette Romance

Please address questions and book requests to:
Silhouette Reader Service
U.S.: 3010 Walden Ave., P.O. Box 1325, Buffalo, NY 14269
Canadian: P.O. Box 609, Fort Erie, Ont. L2A 5X3

LONE STAR RANCHER

Leanna Wilson

ROMANCE™

Published by Silhouette Books

America's Publisher of Contemporary Romance

SILHOUETTE BOOKS

ISBN 0-373-19231-2

LONE STAR RANCHER

Copyright © 1997 by Leanna Ellis

This edition published by arrangement with Harlequin Books S.A.

® and TM are trademarks of Harlequin Books S.A., used under license. Trademarks indicated with ® are registered in the United States Patent and Trademark Office, the Canadian Trade Marks Office and in other countries.

Printed in U.S.A.

Books by Leanna Wilson

Silhouette Romance

Strong, Silent Cowboy #1179
Christmas in July #1197
Lone Star Rancher #1231

LEANNA WILSON

grew up in Dallas, Texas, and taught elementary school for five years. When the writing bug bit her, she quit teaching to write full-time. Always fascinated with rodeos—and cowboys—her first book features one of these strong, silent men. A winner of Romance Writers of America's Golden Heart Award, she lives with her strong, not-so-silent husband in Irving, Texas. Newly married, Gary and Leanna are still honeymooning with their babies—a black Shih Tzu named Muffet and a blond one named Belle.

Chapter One

Tamara Lambert's nose twitched. She drew a shallow breath and sneezed.

"Damn." She hated this ranch. Hated every cow, every rotted fence post, every blasted cow patty. She hated Texas, with its windmills, oil wells and slow-talking, hat-tipping cowboys. She felt like a prisoner, locked behind barbed-wire fences on a worthless piece of land.

Leaning forward once more, she gritted her teeth. "Come on, you old worthless bucket of metal. Start."

The rusty tractor emitted a feeble groan, croaked and died again. Between this tractor and the cantankerous pickup truck, nothing seemed to work around here. Climbing off her perch on the cracked seat, Tamara trudged to the front of the tractor. The thick mud sucked at the boots she'd found in her grandmother's closet. With her hands clenched, she kicked the tire. Another sneeze, another curse, and she glared at the antique John Deere. If only she could have found the manual to the darn thing, but her grandfather had apparently lacked any organizational skills.

This ranch, the one he'd willed her, looked like a junk-yard of discarded tools. Rusted truck innards lay scattered around the barnyard like bleached skeletal remains. Feed sacks, abandoned in the back of the truck, rustled in the autumn breeze.

Rolling up her shirtsleeves, she searched for a way to open the tractor hood and take a look at the engine. Not that she'd know what was what, but it was better than having an all-out temper tantrum. She had to get the tractor started so she could haul a load of hay into the south pasture.

Only a week ago she'd stood in the bookstore she managed in the small Connecticut town of Glenridge, conversing with the usual Saturday crowd and letting novels carry her away to faraway, fantastic places. She had never imagined Texas in her fantasies.

This ranch required hard labor, dirt under her fingernails and catering to a bunch of smelly cows. Usually her job required ordering bestsellers and discussing the newest literary masterpiece with customers. Hauling hay had never entered her mind. Shell-shocked, she looked forward to the day when she sold the cattle and closed the gates for good.

Only one thing kept her going—her never-give-up, never-give-an-inch Lambert determination. She'd inherited that determination from her father. Jason Lambert had made a fortune all on his own.

She'd inherited the ranch from her grandfather. Joe Lambert had wasted his life here amid cactus and mesquite. He'd scratched out a meager living as a cattle rancher. This place had been the death of him.

She found the latch on the tractor's hood. Rust clamped like a vise around the edges. She grabbed a hammer. Metal clanged against metal, severing the quiet of the early morning. After one final whack, she yanked once more and put all her one hundred and twenty pounds into it.

The latch gave way with a suddenness that made her hand slip. She fell back and landed with a splat in the mud. She stared up at the evil tractor. Frustration burned inside her. Mud soaked through her jeans, and she cursed.

The sound of a squeaky axle caught her attention. A dented maroon pickup jounced along the drive. Perfect timing, she thought, pushing herself to her feet. Dirt, grime and bugs splattered the windshield of the truck and obscured her view of her visitor. Just what she needed—more company. Enough neighbors had dropped by in the last week with their sympathies wrapped in plastic wrap for her to start a bakery. Gritting her teeth, she faced the approaching truck with a lift of her chin and a squaring of her shoulders.

The brakes squealed, and the driver's door creaked open. Long, lean legs, clad in pale, overwashed jeans, came into view. The ends of the jeans had frayed, the white threads snaking across the top of the scuffed leather boots. Sharp spurs jangled, and looked as hard and biting as the rest of the cowboy emerging from the truck.

Tall, rugged and weathered around the edges, he had a lean, wiry torso that made his shoulders seem broad and solid. His sweat-stained cowboy hat shadowed his face, making his features dark and angled and alluring. He didn't look like he'd be the type to bring her brownies or a pineapple upside-down cake.

Her heartbeat quickened before she could take a steadying breath. This was a cowboy. Right off the pages of a history book. His faded jeans, worn boots, leather chaps and spurs were the fashion of the old West.

From the looks of this fellow, he was a cowboy through and through. He carried nothing but his head held high, if not at a cocky angle, and wore a jauntily tilted cowboy hat. He looked as rugged as the Texas hill country. Tamara figured he wanted a job. Boy, did she have one lined up.

She hoped he'd be better than the last cowhand, who'd survived less than a day.

"Good morning," she called.

He walked toward her with a slow-as-molasses swagger, obviously unconcerned about the mud patches and cow manure that made the stretch treacherous for anyone else. "Ma'am," he said, his Texas drawl as thick as his mustache. The deep, mellow sound touched an odd chord in her. "How d'ya do?"

"I'm fine, thank you." She folded her arms over her chest. His direct stare made her nervous.

The conversation came to an abrupt halt, like rush-hour traffic on the Merrit Parkway. She met his gaze. Tiny sun lines creased the corners of his eyes, as if he had a perpetual squint. The brown orbs reflected the fall foliage in the surrounding shrubs and trees, a kaleidoscope of leafy browns, maple reds and golden sunlight. A tinge of homesickness rippled through her. God, how she missed the spectacular Connecticut autumn.

"What can I do for you?" she asked.

He pulled a folded piece of newspaper from his back pocket, and she noticed how his buckskin chaps hugged his slim hips. Diverting her eyes, she met his gaze, and her cheeks warmed.

"Saw your ad." His mouth quirked beneath the canopy of his mustache. "Thought I could help you out."

A sigh escaped her, and she told herself it was because of the possibility of hiring help, not from watching his firm lips move. Nodding, she said, "You're accustomed to ranch work?"

It sounded like a dumb question, but the two college kids she'd hired earlier hadn't known a hoe from a two-by-four.

"Been doing it my whole life. I could give you a few references, if you need 'em."

His slow Texas drawl irritated her. "Maybe." References wouldn't hurt, she figured, after she'd hired that worthless drunk. But those college cowboys had been worse. She was better off without them, but she couldn't risk not hiring someone soon. An idea formed in her mind. "From what I understand," she said, "a foreman has to be able to do almost anything around a ranch."

The man gave a slight nod of agreement.

"More than rope a cow and ride a horse."

He nodded. His gaze roamed over her, assessing her as if she were a cow on the auction block. She received the distinct impression that she didn't measure up to his standards. Whatever those might be. Not that she cared. Her own father had detoured away from his ranch upbringing. Tamara certainly didn't care what this hick cowboy thought about her.

She shifted from foot to foot, and she felt the wet coolness of mud on her backside. She clasped her hands behind her back. "There's a heavy workload that will be required."

His gaze never wavered. "Always is too much work on a ranch. I work till I get the job done."

So, he didn't expect to punch a time clock. This was a different world from the one she'd been raised in back east, and running this ranch differed considerably from managing a store of employees. But she liked his attitude.

And she liked his athletic build...er...his muscular frame looked like he could do just about anything he wanted. His solid, thick shoulders bunched with the slightest movement. He had a workingman's hands, rough, callused, strong. The hands of this cowboy were his résumé. He had a rider's legs, with solid thigh muscles that produced a determined, no-nonsense gait. She figured this cowboy had a good... seat.

Something sizzled inside her, but she quickly convinced herself her interest was purely innocent. From her time riding Thoroughbreds, she recognized a rider when she saw one. It was important that he could sit a horse well. She shook loose those scintillating thoughts. A good seat, after all, was a necessary asset for a ranch foreman.

She would never be interested in a cowboy for anything other than that.

"I tell you what," she said, feeling nervous twitters in her stomach, "if you can get this tractor to start, then you can have the job." If he chose not to take it, after he saw how much work was required, then at least she'd have the tractor running.

His gaze flicked over the John Deere. "Sure thing, ma'am."

Without another word, he stepped forward and climbed aboard, as if mounting a horse. Watching him, she couldn't imagine that he'd ever back away from a difficult task. Almost like her father going into negotiations to buy another company. She admired determination and confidence.

This cowboy's shoulder and arm muscles bulged as he worked the gears and tried the ignition. In a few minutes, without one curse word, he turned the ignition, and the tractor came to life.

"How did you do that?" she asked, amazed at his skill.

"Just have to know how to hold your mouth right."

Bewildered by his statement, she raised her eyebrows.

"That's an old saying around here."

With a somber look, he glanced down at her. "Guess this means I've got the job."

She sensed at that moment his need for a job might match hers to hire someone quick. "Well, you did start the tractor."

A hint of a smile pulled at his mouth, and a sensation that she didn't recognize or understand curled inside her. Then he ducked his head, as if contemplating whether to take it or not. She hoped he would, because, frankly, she didn't have many cowboys knocking on her door. But she wouldn't give in and offer more money. "The offer I made in the paper is all I can afford to pay."

"That sounds fair." He stared straight at her, his eyes as dark as the end of her grandfather's double-barreled shotgun. "Figure there's something you ought to know first."

Wariness arced through her. What now? Maybe he wanted to have every Saturday and Sunday off, like those college cowboys. Uncertain, she waited for him to continue, wanting to hold firm, but already willing to capitulate in order to get some help.

"I've got two kids." He rushed on to say, "They won't give you any trouble. If you decide to hire me, that is."

That was it? It wasn't what she'd expected, but she figured it could be worse. His statement doused her simmering thoughts. This man had a family. A wife. Children. Two, to be exact.

That was good, wasn't it? She ignored the disappointment that wafted through her. As an only child, she'd never been around other children much. She'd always been more comfortable in the adult world. But these children wouldn't get in her way. This could be better than she'd imagined. His wife could care for the children, leaving the cowboy free to be dependable and responsible. Which fit her needs.

"Your children shouldn't be a problem," she said. "You and your wife can live in—"

"I don't have a wife."

Something sparked inside her again, like kindling rubbed together to create a fire. Dousing her out-of-the-blue interest with a bucket of reality, she reminded herself that this was a *cowboy*. Plain and simple. He was from a different world. One she didn't like at all. Quite frankly, he wasn't her type.

She liked silk and pearls.

He liked leather and spurs.

In spite of her decided disinterest in him as a man, questions spiraled through her mind. Why did a sadness lurk in the depths of his eyes? Had his wife left him with two children? Had he suffered through a divorce? Sympathy tugged at her heart. But she squashed it. What did she care about this cowboy and his troubles? She had her own worries. And she needed his help.

Finally she asked, "How old are your children?"

"They're old enough. Pretty self-sufficient. Old enough to go to school and keep themselves out of trouble."

Disappointment crept through her. Somehow she'd expected more from this cowboy. Suddenly she wanted to grab him by the shirt and tell him that children needed their parents. Children needed love. Whoever heard of self-sufficient children?

Wasn't that her own parents' attitude? She'd gone from a latchkey kid to a boarding school brat. But she'd learned to take care of herself. Her parents had taught her independence, given it to her as a gift.

Cooling her heated thoughts with a slow breath, she realized that how this cowboy raised his children was not her concern. Whether he could do the job was.

"I figured," the cowboy continued, "that I'd give each of them a chore or two around the ranch. Teach 'em a little responsibility. Teach 'em about cattle and ranching."

She'd expected that much. "Just don't forget the responsibility is yours."

"I don't shirk my responsibilities." The glint in his brown eyes told her he spoke the truth.

Maybe this cowboy had potential after all. As a father, that is. His traditional values and old-fashioned ideas seemed to go well with his out-of-the-century outfit. Blocking out those thoughts, she said, "I suppose your children won't be too much of a problem, then. You'll stay in the guest cottage.'' She hooked her thumb over her shoulder toward the main house, and the smaller version set off to the side. ''There's plenty of room there.''

''Okay,'' he said. He climbed off the tractor and stuck out his hand. ''It's a deal, then.''

She meant to give him a cool, distancing fingertip handshake, but his hand clasped hers, engulfing her smaller one. For a second, she felt vulnerable. His palm flattened against hers, and she felt the rough, sandpapery texture of his flesh. A shocking warmth vibrated between their two hands.

Her gaze locked with his for a second too long. A second that made her feel as if he'd taken a peek into her soul. A second when awareness sprang up between them. A shock wave rippled up her arm. As if she'd been jolted by a charge of electricity, she pulled her hand away. Trying to erase the sensation, she rubbed her palm against the back of her jeans and ended up with a muddy hand.

''There's one problem.'' Her voice sounded strained. Her heart pounded. She took a step backward, as if he'd breached an invisible line.

His warm gaze remained on her, like the pressure of a hand on her shoulder. His brow arched toward a shock of dark brown hair that curled enticingly across his forehead.

She swallowed. Part of her wanted to run from this man. It was an inexplicable feeling. Her logical side dismissed it, and her desperation overruled all doubts and worries. ''I don't even know your name.''

He tilted his hat in a salute. ''Clint Morgan, ma'am.''

''I'm Tamara Lambert.'' She managed a half smile. Her insides squirmed as he continued to stare at her. Irritated at him, she said, ''I'd appreciate it if you'd quit calling me 'ma'am.'''

''Yes'm.'' He shrugged. ''Old habit.''

She noted that he didn't apologize. She tapped down her annoyance. Most Texans used the Southern formalities, addressing waitresses and female doctors alike as ''sugar'' and ''ma'am'' and ''little lady.'' Cowboy condescension. It made her nerves prickle.

Feeling the heat of his gaze on her, she brushed her fingers through her hair and said, ''I suppose it's settled, then. Come on, I'll give you a mini tour around the ranch.''

''Yes'm, but...''

She paused. Now what?

''I figured you needed this bale hauled.''

''Well, that's true.'' This time she gave him a wider, more appreciative smile. If he wanted to work, she'd give him plenty of it. ''When are your children arriving?''

''Whenever it's convenient for you. They're at a motel in Georgetown. It's only a ten- or fifteen-minute drive from here. I figured when I finished with my chores, I'd pick them up and get them settled.''

''Okay, then. After the hay, why don't you bring them on over, and I'll give all of you a tour?''

''Yes'm. That'll be just fine.''

A spark of hope ignited inside her. This was a professional cowboy. A man she would be able to count on. Work came first with him. She liked that. She liked him. As a foreman, that is.

He would help her restore the ranch to full working order so that she could sell it. Then, like Dorothy in Oz, she'd click her grandmother's boot heels together and get back East.

The color of the leaves had begun to change from a deep green to gold and russet, carpeting the ground around Annie Purl Elementary School. Fall had arrived in the Texas hill country, bringing a shift in temperature. A weathered rope hung from a live-oak branch, the tire at the bottom twisting and turning with the rhythm of the wind. Tied by a rope of responsibility and painful memories, Clint wrestled with giving up his freedom.

He pulled into the empty parking lot and stared at the playground. Memories tugged at him, pulling him back across the years. He'd played here with his brother, Neal. Now his niece played here, with her kindergarten class. It was for her that he was doing this. For Mandy and Ryan both.

Before being hobbled by responsibilities, Clint hadn't stayed long in one place, moving from ranch to ranch, to whatever outfit would keep him in the saddle from sunup to sundown. He was a rover. He preferred it that way. He liked to see new countryside, toss his bedroll on a forgotten piece of dirt and throw in with an outfit that would keep him on the open range.

His kind of cowboying was hard to find these days, what with newfangled tractors and enterprises that used two-wheelers and helicopters to track a herd. But some places a helicopter couldn't fight the wind. Some places a motor-bike couldn't travel the rugged terrain. But a good stock horse and a well-seasoned cowboy could.

Now, that life of his was over.

The life he'd clung to, chased after, chosen. The life his father, grandfather and great-grandfather had led as cow-boys living on the wide-open range, until they all married and settled down. Clint had promised himself he wouldn't surrender his freedom. He'd held on to the callus-making, hard-driving, backbreaking life he loved.

But like an old oak tree struck by a sudden crack of lightning, his life had been split in two, singed by reality, burned by responsibility.

This job as ranch foreman would be different from any other he'd ever held. It had to be. For the first time in his life, he needed it to be permanent.

He squinted against the red glare of the sun. Rolling

down the truck's window, he drew in a deep breath of the
fresh, clean air, holding it inside him, as if it were his last
taste of freedom. The rugged land to the southwest called
to him, tempted him as a man might be tempted by lush,
feminine curves and a warm, enticing smile. But this time
he had to decline the horizon's seduction. Clint resolved to
set aside his old way of life and face the new...dif-
ferent...confining life ahead of him.

He shoved the gearshift into drive and headed toward the
motel to pick up the kids. When he reached the room, he
found Mandy all alone. Anger shot through him.

"Where's Ryan?" His voice boomed in the confines of
the small room.

The little girl's blue eyes widened. Her hat drooped over
her eyes, giving her all the dignity of a Munchkin. "He
went to get a cold drink."

"Well, he shouldn't have left you alone."

"I can take care of myself, Uncle Clint." She drew herself up, squaring her shoulders. She gave him a tentative
smile, but her blue eyes remained wide, with a spark of
uncertainty in them. "Did you get the job?"

He nodded. "Yep. We've got to load our stuff in the
pickup. We're going to live on a ranch. And you can stay
in your kindergarten class."

Without a word, she scooted off the bed and collected
her herd of plastic horses. Carefully she placed them in an
old shoe box and closed the lid. Clint carried a load of
suitcases and settled them in the bed of the pickup. Mandy
followed him. Her white-blond hair glistened in the morning light as she put her box on the front seat.

The five-year-old retraced her footsteps, her dirt-brown
boots scuffing along the sidewalk. She wore baggy jeans
and a faded checkered shirt, leftovers from her older
brother. When Clint first came back to Texas six months
ago, after his brother's fatal accident, he'd offered to buy

Mandy a frilly lace dress, but his niece had preferred jeans to satin bows. A smile tugged at the corner of Clint's mouth. God, how she reminded him of his brother. Clint's chest tightened, and he blinked back the memories.

Clint knotted a rope over the load of toys and suitcases piled up like the Beverly Hillbillies' truck. It took another thirty minutes before Ryan sauntered back toward the room.

He scowled at his teenage nephew. "Where have you been?"

Ryan held up a red can of cola, then slurped down the contents.

"You should have stayed with Mandy, like I told you."

The fifteen-year-old shrugged. "I'm not her baby-sitter."

Clint bit back a harsh retort. He didn't know what he'd do with his brother's firstborn. Ryan had experienced a lot of changes in his life over the past few months. Clint had to cut him some slack. Maybe their new home, a permanent one, would help his nephew's attitude. He hoped so, anyway, because Clint's nerves were as sharp as barbed wire.

They arrived in midafternoon at the Bar L Ranch, and his new boss was waiting on the porch for them. Now her clothes matched her refined, dignified accent. Tamara had exchanged her muddy jeans, work shirt and oversize boots for pleated slacks and a fuzzy sweater, which were about as useful on a ranch as high heels. She looked untouchable, with her long, dark hair slicked back in place. She didn't look like she belonged on any ranch he'd ever worked. What had he gotten himself into?

His shoulder muscles tightened. He didn't need a woman whose Yankee accent raked across him like spur rowels. Though he didn't have much choice. Foreman positions were hard to find. But what did a Yankee know about ranching? How would he manage with a female boss? Shrugging off his doubts, he figured he'd be running things, anyway. To him, Tamara Lambert didn't seem too inclined to ranching. With a chuckle, he remembered her muddy backside, but then a tightness in his groin choked off his laughter.

"Hello," she called as she walked toward the truck. She sidestepped a mud puddle in her citified shoes.

Clint raised a finger from the steering wheel in greeting and set his jaw. "Y'all behave now," he said to the kids before his boss got too close to the pickup. "She's my boss, and she's given us a place to live, so put on your best Sunday-go-to-meetin' manners. Understand?"

Mandy nodded. She stared up at him with solemn blue eyes.

Ryan rolled his eyes with that too-familiar teenage rebelliousness. He slumped against the passenger door, a bored expression on his face.

Shaking his head, Clint opened the creaky door and tipped the brim of his hat toward Tamara Lambert. Her blue eyes crinkled with a welcoming smile. Something inside him buzzed, and he ignored it like it was a pesky fly.

Mandy followed him out of the truck, her hand grasping one of his belt loops. He reached down and lifted her into his arms. She hooked an arm around his neck. It sent an odd sensation through him to have this little girl depend on him, not only for food and shelter, but also for emotional support. A warmth filled him, like hot coffee on a frosty morning.

"This is Mandy," he said to his boss.

Tamara smiled at the little girl. It was a warm smile that made his gaze linger for a second too long on her generous mouth. "Hello, Mandy. Welcome to the Bar L Ranch."

Mandy peeked at her through thick blond lashes.

"How old are you?" Tamara asked, moving closer.

His niece glanced at him, and he nodded to her. "Go ahead. Tell her." He patted her back. "It's okay."

Without looking at Tamara, Mandy held up five fingers.

"My goodness," his Yankee boss said, "you must already be in kindergarten. I bet you're good at helping your daddy...."

She bucked, and shook her head, her pigtails whirling like windmills. "He's not my daddy."

A flash of pain shot through Clint. She was right—he wasn't her father. No one could replace his brother, Neal. As quickly as the pain flared, he shuttered his emotions. He met Tamara's curious stare. "I'm her uncle."

"Oh... I'm sorry, I thought..." Tamara stammered. Her gaze softened, turning her blue eyes into pools of sympathy. "Mandy, you must be good at helping your uncle Clint, then."

This time his niece nodded and wrapped her arms tighter around his neck. Instinctively he tightened his arm about Mandy's waist. He didn't know much about little girls, but he'd learned Mandy needed frequent hugs. Holding her often worked better than words. Ryan, on the other hand, was a whole different matter.

"What's your name?" Tamara asked, turning her attention to his nephew, who had slid into the driver's seat.

Ryan heaved a bored sigh and looked away.

Clint shot him an irritated look. "Answer the lady."

The teen rolled his eyes, but this time said, "Ryan."

"He's a typical teenager," Clint apologized, scowling at his nephew. "Or so his teachers say."

"He's always in a bad mood," Mandy added.

"I see," Tamara said. "Well, you're all welcome here. Let me show you where you'll be staying." She turned toward the cottage and took the lead.

Clint herded the kids, keeping a few paces back from his new boss. Tamara was tall, and willowy-thin, but he sensed she was unbreakable, with a purpose and drive to match her long stride. She had the confidence of a ranch owner, yet the awkwardness of an ungainly colt.

He'd seen her working on the tractor, seen her fall on her backside, heard her cuss a blue streak. In that Yankee accent of hers. Her temper had made him smile. So had her cute backside, covered with mud. He'd noticed, even though she'd tried to keep her back turned away from him. Her slim body offered curves no cowboy should have, but that any cowboy could damn well appreciate. Clint averted his gaze, uneasiness slipping around him like a hangman's knot.

His gaze swept the cottage. A porch spanned the front of the house. Along the windowsill, the withered stems of petunias and marigolds shriveled in flowerpots. One shutter hung crooked on its hinges, its paint chipped and cracked with age.

Carrying Mandy on his hip, Clint climbed the three wooden steps and crossed the porch and threshold. His eyes widened in the dim light, but focused on the clean hardwood floors and the simple yet adequate furnishings. In the front room, a lumpy couch and a small television occupied the limited space. A breakfast table almost filled the tiny kitchen.

"Ryan, unload the stuff from the truck and watch your little sister." Clint gave his nephew a meaningful glance and set Mandy on the floor. "I'd like to take a look at the barn and speak with Miz Lambert here about the ranch."

A few minutes later, Clint leaned against the fence and stared out at a corral that held a good-size Angus bull with wide, muscular shoulders and thick, stocky legs. He remembered Old Joe Lambert, remembered the old man's pride, the old man's gumption. For his memory, Clint wanted to make this place what it had once been.

"Your niece and nephew seem nice," Tamara said.

"They're good kids."

"There's a lot of years between them, though."

Clint nodded. "Yeah. When Ryan turned ten, my sister-in-law and brother decided they wanted another baby. They thought they'd managed pretty well with one. And Ryan hadn't caught the disease yet."

Her eyes widened into deep blue pools of alarm. "Disease?"

He grinned. "It's not catching to those who've already been through puberty."

"Ah," she said. "Teenageitis."

He nodded. "But two proved more difficult work."

"Yes, I can understand that. At least, it's the same with cows." Her gaze flicked toward the herd munching on grass on the open range. "The ranch needs a lot of work. I've ordered some paint for the house."

His head snapped toward her. Women. All they thought about was redecorating, instead of the practicalities of life.

"It should be here early in the week. I'd like you to begin painting right away."

He clamped his jaw shut. What the hell did she think he was? A yard boy? He was a *cowboy*. He rode horses and took care of cows. Maybe she didn't know what a ranch foreman did.

"Excuse me, Miz Lambert. But don't you think my focus should be the cattle? There's a lot of work to do with them. Vaccinations. Breeding. I gotta turn this old boy—" he pointed toward the bull "—out to pasture."

Her brow furrowed. "Why? He's fine where he is."

He hooked his thumb in his front pocket. He realized he was treading on difficult terrain that could embarrass the heck out of him or her or both of them. The blunt language he would have used with a male boss stuck in his throat. "He's got his own job to do. He's gotta kick up his heels with the ladies. If you know what I mean."

She blushed, a pink hue darkening her cheeks. "But I need the houses painted. That's the most important task at the moment."

He squared his shoulders and turned toward her. "Begging your pardon, ma'am—" he let that linger between them, which seemed to make her stiffen with irritation "—but if we don't let this old bull do his job, then we won't have any calves next year. That's how a ranch makes money. Selling calves."

"You don't have to be condescending," she snapped. "I know how a ranch makes money. And how it doesn't." She frowned. "But we won't be keeping the herd."

"What?" he asked, dumbfounded.

"If the ranch and cattle won't sell as a complete package, then we'll sell everything separately. Whichever will be more profitable."

"What?" The word exploded from his throat.

"I'd like to have everything sold around the first of the year. That's when I have to be back east. My job would only give me so much time off. Even unpaid."

Clint's heart slammed to a stop. That wasn't his plan. He'd be out of work. Then the kids would have to move. Again. "Let me get this straight." He strapped his rising frustration down. "You hired me to fix up the ranch so you can sell it?"

"Yes. You didn't think I wanted to stay here, did you?"

"I just assumed…" He stopped himself. He'd obviously assumed wrong. Damn. "It's your grandfather's ranch. Don't you want to hold on to it?"

"No."

Appalled, he kept a tight rein on his tongue. Didn't family matter to her? He'd lost enough to know that nothing else mattered. Even dreams. No matter how he longed for the open range and his roving life, he wouldn't abandon his family. They came first. Tamara's disregard for her grandfather's gift aggravated him.

"Didn't he leave the ranch to you?" he asked.

"Yes." She glanced away.

"Instead of to your father?" he persisted, aiming at the rumors that had run rampant through town about how Old Joe Lambert had overlooked his own son in his will.

Her gaze slammed into his. "The specifications of my grandfather's will are none of your business."

"I suppose that's true. But losing my job *is* my business, lady. Don't you want to make a go of it here?"

"I'm going home," she said. "Back to Connecticut."

He drew a deep breath and let it out slowly. His hopes for making this a permanent home for the kids, a safe, secure environment, came tumbling down around him.

Chapter Two

With his thumbs hooked in his front pockets, Clint walked the path from the barn to the house. The whine of an eighteen-wheeler drew his attention, and its headlights slashed across a billboard-size sign. He stopped and stared. The For Sale sign loomed perpendicular to the highway, big enough for Oklahomans to see, some two hundred miles to the north. Sometime in the last couple of hours Tamara had stuck the sign in the yard. He imagined every trucker, tourist or passerby who drove the two-lane road jotting down the phone number.

His stomach knotted with irritation. All day he'd tried to forget the announcement that Tamara had made yesterday. He'd blatantly ignored her request to begin fixing up the house. He'd stuck to what he knew best—cattle. He'd turned out the Angus bull into a pasture filled with cows, fixed a loose fence post and separated the heifers and young bulls from their mamas. He'd worked hard, and his muscles ached. But this For Sale sign felt like a slap in the face. A reminder that he'd failed to provide the kids with a secure home life.

The minutes in the day had sped past, until now the sun dipped low on the horizon, casting the ranch in a flattering glow of orange light. Darkness shadowed the corners and shrubs around the cottage house. He noticed the flickering crack of light through the curtains as he walked up the steps and knew the kids were watching television.

Sighing, he stretched the kinks out of his shoulders and scraped the mud off his boots. He dropped his spurs on the porch with a clatter. As his mind churned with a list of all that needed to be done tomorrow, he realized that every chore he accomplished, every fence post he fixed, brought him closer to the moment when Tamara Lambert would sell this place.

When he'd be out of a job. And a home.

Maybe he shouldn't have taken the position, if it meant moving in another couple of months, or however long it would take to sell. But he'd shaken hands on it. He remembered that startled feeling shooting through him when he'd touched Tamara's hand. Her palm had been softer than he'd imagined, much softer than her grating Yankee accent.

How could she not care about her own family's land? What was so important about going back to Connecticut? Did she have a better life there? Clint couldn't imagine anything better than owning land, living on it and making it yield. Then a thought occurred to him, and an odd twinge of disappointment followed on its footsteps. Maybe she had someone, a boyfriend, a lover, back there. She could even be married. Some women didn't take their husband's names. Some newfangled women's-lib bull. Maybe she had someone to return home to.

Swiping his shirtsleeve across his forehead, he focused on the most probable reason. Tamara Lambert hated Texas. And she plainly didn't like being a rancher, either.

Which left him as discouraged as a sad-eyed hound dog.

Shrugging off his melancholy, he opened the door to the

cottage, ready to resume his role as guardian. Shrieks and
gunshots greeted him. The volume on the television had
been cranked too high, and Ryan sat on the couch, watching
a Bruce Willis movie with explosions echoing in the room.
Mandy, red-faced and fists clenched, took a swing at him.
Her brother held her at arm's length with his palm against
her forehead. Clint's nerves snapped.

Mandy stopped her struggles and ran for him. "Ryan
was being mean. You know what he did?"

Grappling with his frustration, Clint shook his head, patted the little girl's shoulder and hollered over the commo-
tion, "Turn the TV down, Ryan! Now!"

Finally, the teen, his gaze glued to the tube, grabbed the
remote. The boy took his time lowering the volume, and
Clint glared at him until it reached an acceptable level.
Clint frowned. This father thing was rough, and he didn't
think he was doing a very good job at it.

"Uncle Clint..." Mandy tugged on his shirt. "Ryan
was..."

"Shh..." He was already tired of the bickering, his
nerves stretched taut. He wanted to come home to the warm
family environment he'd known as a kid. He and his
brother, although they fought once in a while, had been
pals. There'd only been two years between them. Yeah,
they'd wrestled good-naturedly, making Clint tough enough
to whip any boy in his own class and wrangle steers in the
high school rodeo, but there had always been a bond between them. Love had never been talked about, never
thought of, but it had been there. Strong and durable as a
good rope.

So, what was wrong with these kids? What was wrong
with him? At the moment, he wasn't feeling an abundance
of love for either of them. But he knew the reason for the
chaos. They'd all been through a lot in the past few months,
losing their parents, moving away from their friends. Then

Clint's mother had died, and that had stripped him of any-body to lean on and taken the last of his savings. Clint realized then that he hadn't had much success holding this family together. Where was the understanding, the respect, the love?

"Ryan," he said, exasperated and guilt-ridden, "apolo-gize to your little sister."

"But—"

"Do it."

Shrugging, Ryan mumbled, "Sorry."

"Okay." Clint tried a weak smile. "Let's fix supper. Mandy, get the corn bread out of the refrigerator."

Her lower lip protruded. "I'm tired of that."

Clint's nerves shredded. "Too bad."

Who was he trying to fool? He wasn't a father. These kids needed a real parent, someone who had the patience and ability to understand and relate to them. They needed more than food, water and shelter. They needed emotional support and guidance. Most of all, they needed love, and he didn't know if he could provide all they deserved.

Guilt wrapped around his soul. He'd sworn to his brother and these kids that he'd take care of them. He had a duty. One that he wouldn't turn his back on. Ever.

But his new responsibility made him feel totally alone.

Tamara tromped through the mud toward the barn. Even the bright, crisp day, full of sunshine and autumn scents, couldn't sweeten her sour mood.

When she reached the corral, she leaned against the weathered boards and said, "What are you doing?"

Clint glanced over his shoulder. He was kneeling beside a metal chute. The bawling calf looked pitiful, unable to move while Clint jabbed it with a needle. Despite the cool weather, Clint had removed his sheepskin jacket and laid it over the fence rails. "I'm working the calves."

She ignored the way his muscles bunched beneath his plaid shirt as he released a lever. The little calf shot out of the metal jaws like he'd been poked with a cattle prod. Anger burned inside her. "I thought I asked you to fix—"

"Yes, ma'am, but these calves needed worming and vaccinations."

His attitude irked her. Who was the boss around here? "Even if we're gonna sell them?"

"Yes'm." His jaw tightened. "If they're sickly, they won't pull high dollar. I didn't think you'd want me to take the chance that they might get a disease that could get the ranch quarantined."

"Quarantined?" She choked on the word.

He nodded. "If they were to catch something, we could get quarantined up to three years. That'd stop a sale of the ranch for sure. I found the vaccinations in the barn there, as if your grandpa was planning on doing it soon." He glanced down at the ground, his cowboy hat shadowing his face. Finally, he looked back at her and shrugged. "Their health seemed more important than scraping old paint off the side of the house."

She gritted her teeth. She had no argument against what he'd said. "Well, get to it as fast as you can."

"Yes, ma'am." He tipped his hat. She wondered if it was more a mocking gesture than a polite courtesy.

Clenching her hands into tight fists, she ignored his calling her "ma'am." She wouldn't pick another fight with him. Somehow she always seemed to lose arguments with him, anyway. He seemed so narrow-minded. Just like her grandfather. But Clint never got angry. He had an even temper, unlike her father. But he vexed her anyway. She turned on her heel and headed back to the house. She had to start packing up her grandfather's things.

"Miz Lambert," he called.

She faced him again, her patience as thin as an eggshell.

"We're running a little low on feed."

She sighed. Another expense. Running the ranch cost more money than she'd ever imagined. No wonder her grandfather had scratched out such a meager living here. "How much do we need?"

"Depends," he said in his slow Southern drawl.

"On what?"

"On how long you want to stock up for."

Optimistic she'd sell soon, she said, "Let's take it a month at a time."

He nodded, and his mouth thinned into a grim line. "Yes'm. I'll drive over to the feed store this afternoon and take care of things."

Something in his tone irritated her. She folded her arms over her chest. "I'll go with you."

That way, she could see he didn't goof off. She could get him back here in time to start preparing the house. The paint should arrive soon.

"Whatever you wanna do, Miz Lambert." His heavy-lidded gaze knotted her insides.

Before she could respond, he turned his back on her and moved the next calf into the metal chute. He bent over and studied the calf, the lines of his back molded by his flannel shirt. His chaps hugged his hips and flared out along his thighs, accentuating his lean hardness. A cool breeze ruffled Tamara's hair, yet inside her jacket she tingled with a prickly heat.

She zipped up her windbreaker and headed toward the house, determined to show this insolent cowboy who was boss. He would start getting her house ready to paint, without any more excuses.

Throughout the rest of the morning, she watched Clint work from the warmth of her kitchen window. While she folded her grandfather's clothes and packed them in boxes, Clint never stopped moving, never paused for a break, never quit. Until his task was done. Finally, late in the afternoon, he knocked on the front door and told her he was ready to head to the feed store.

Again, he'd told *her* what to do, not the other way around. Frustration built inside her like a gathering storm. She climbed into the cab of her grandfather's truck and started the ignition. It moaned and sputtered mutinously, much like Clint deciding what *he* wanted to do, rather than following her instructions.

She cursed.

He chuckled. "Give the gas pedal a little pump."

"What?" She frowned at him.

He reached over and laid a hand over hers, making her fingers tingle. He turned off the ignition. "Now, pump the gas pedal a few times."

Unable to draw a deep breath, she did as he said.

"That's enough. Now, try it again." With his hand still on hers, he turned the ignition key, and the motor caught.

Suddenly, she was very much aware of his presence, pressing in and suffocating her. But he wasn't within two feet of her. Still, his hot, appraising gaze made her insides squirm. She had the urge to wipe that smirk off his face. But she didn't know how she'd even try.

Shoving the gearshift into first, she gunned the engine, and the truck lurched forward. Clint came out of his seat and nearly collided with the dashboard. She gripped the steering wheel, her knuckles turning white. Keeping her eyes on the road, she ignored him.

The silence in the cab felt like a cold chill. She could hear his slow, deep breaths and imagined him laughing at her. Her nerves twisted into irritated coils. To break the silence and hopefully the tension, she said, "Ms. Cooper, the real estate agent, is bringing a couple out on Saturday to see the ranch."

"Hmm." Clint sounded gruff, like an angry bear. He

stared straight ahead. His profile looked stern, almost majestic, like the rim of a mountain range set against the sky. The curve of his dark mustache made it seem as if he were frowning, and the brim of his hat cast shadows across his face, making his skin a darker shade of tan, and more menacing. His stubborn determination matched the knife-edged slope of his nose and the squared set of his jaw.

With his help, if she could get him to prepare and paint the house, then maybe they could sell the ranch. Then it hit her. Maybe that was why he didn't want to help. Maybe he was trying to sabotage her efforts to sell out. He had seemed irritated when she told him her plans.

No matter what his problem, he worked for her. And he'd do what she told him and paid him to do. They had five days to get the house painted. When paint arrived tomorrow, she'd put the paintbrush in his hand.

But today she had another chore. She steered the truck onto the main highway. "How much food do you think we need?"

Clint studied her, his eyes steady and intense. He seemed to notice everything with those deep brown eyes. His steady, unwavering gaze made her insides quiver with an awkward anticipation. Although she kept her eyes trained on the road, she was very much aware of Clint, sitting two feet away from her, close enough to reach out and touch.... If she dared. But she didn't.

"Probably about a hundred bags of feed. We have enough hay behind the barn to last for a long while, if not all the way through the winter. We need a few sacks of grain and rolled oats for the horses."

She remembered watching the two horses grazing in the pasture, their coats thick for the coming winter. It had brought back memories of riding Thoroughbreds and the freedom she'd experienced jumping fences. What would it be like now to race across one of her own pastures, the wind whipping at her, the horse lunging beneath her? But Texas held no allure for her, only bad memories.

Keeping that in mind, she drove the rest of the way in silence, her thoughts centered on finding a buyer for the ranch. She parked beside the Worms and Minnows 4 Sale sign at Earl's Feed Store. Zipping her jacket against the wind, she climbed out of the truck and noticed that Clint's sheepskin jacket remained open. He seemed unaffected by the cold, just as he always seemed impervious to anything around him and undaunted by hard work.

As they approached the ramshackle building, he jogged past her and held the door open for her to enter first. She hesitated, staring at him. It was a courtesy she hadn't expected or wanted, and she wasn't sure whether she appreciated it or not. Giving him a terse smile, she ducked her head and walked over the threshold into the store. A warmth settled over her, and she thanked the floor heater with the angry red coils.

"Hey, there, Clint!"

"Earl." Clint greeted the owner, who stood behind the sales counter. "How're you doin'?"

"Fine, long as I stay right here." He sipped his coffee, his large hand seeming to engulf the foam cup. "Too damn cold out there today. Gonna be one heck of a winter."

"Sure is," Clint agreed. "Earl, this here's my new ranch boss, Miz Tamara Lambert."

One strap of the older gentleman's overalls had fallen forward. "Why, I'll be hornswoggled!" His sharp blue eyes narrowed on Tamara. "You Old Joe's granddaughter?"

"Yes, I am." An odd sensation rippled through her at the excitement twinkling in Earl's eyes at the mention of her grandfather.

"Heckfire!" He slapped his hand on the counter and

nearly spilt his coffee out of the other hand. "Little Tammy Jo!"

Her mouth fell open. Earl had used the name her grandfather had once preferred. She hated the sound of it. It had no class, no dignity. It sounded like a hick name some barefoot backwoods brat would have. Catching Clint studying her with a sly grin, she clamped her mouth shut. Heat rose to her cheeks, and suddenly the store felt too small and way too hot.

Pleased with himself, Earl grinned like a slice of fresh-cut watermelon. "Heck, I remember the day you was born. Old Joe was so proud. He strutted in here, having just come from that hospital over in Austin, and told us all about you. He acted like a peacock, all puffed up at having held his only grandbaby. Said you looked just like him, and I'm relieved to know Old Joe lied. You're a sight better-lookin' than that old coot.

"Why, Joe used to talk about his little Tammy Jo all the time. Couldn't get the old feller to talk about anything else, especially when he'd get one of your school pictures your mama sent. Why, he'd whip out his wallet and show everybody and anybody who'd pay attention long enough."

Earl's features sobered. "I surely am sorry about your loss, miss. I thought the world of your grandpa." He shook his head, as if trying to deal with his own pain. "Real shame it was to lose such a fine gentleman. Real shame."

The moment ballooned. Tamara shifted from foot to foot, unsure what to say. She hadn't known her grandfather, hadn't seen him since she was six years old. The memories stuck her like cacti. The arguments between her grandfather and father had been thick with strife and resentment. Moving to Connecticut had eased the tension in her family.

Although she'd never seen her grandfather again, she remembered the anger and bitterness in her father toward his parent. Earl's fond memories seemed to contradict the image of the man engraved in her own mind—Old Joe's hard-as-granite gray eyes, glaring at her father.

"He was a tough old bugger," Earl said, his voice lighter.

"Sure was," Clint added.

Tamara imagined they thought she was fighting tears over her grandfather's death. Instead, she was trying desperately to feel something. Anything but this emptiness. How could she feel sorrow for a man she'd never known? Her father had severed those family ties years ago, and they no longer had any pull on her.

"Remember when Joe caught himself with a lure?" Clint asked.

Earl nodded. "Yep. He came by here. Held out his hand. There that sucker was. He'd caught himself, all right."

Perplexing emotions swirled through Tamara as she listened to these men speak of her grandfather like some lost hero. Old Joe, as they called him, had obviously been loved and respected. But not by his one son. Obviously the strife had been two-way, since her grandfather had left his son nothing in his will.

Earl chuckled. "I said to him, 'Joe, ain't ya s'posed to throw one of them lures in the water to catch a bass?' And Old Joe just said, 'I caught what I wanted to catch. Now cut the damn thing out, Earl.'"

Tamara stiffened at Earl's wheezing laughter. She glanced at Clint and saw a wry grin curving his mouth. "Didn't you send for a doctor?"

"Nah," Earl answered. "Your grandpa didn't care none for doctors. He figured, since I could doctor my horses, then I could fix him up. So, I cut it out with my huntin' knife here." He slapped his hip, where a six-inch blade was encased in leather along his side. "And Old Joe didn't flinch once. Not once. He was tough, your grandpa was. Real tough."

Tamara swallowed, unsure how to react to this piece of news. "Yes, well—"

"So, I guess y'all didn't come all this way to jaw." Earl rubbed his rounded belly. "What'd'ya need, Clint?"

Tamara bristled at Earl's assumption that Clint was in charge. She was the owner. She had the checkbook. "I'll take care of it."

Both men looked at her, and her confidence faltered. "Um, we need a hundred feed bags."

Wasn't that what Clint had said? She refused to look in his direction.

"What kind of feed, Tammy Jo?" Earl asked.

Bristling, she said, "Cow food."

Clint chuckled, and she shot him an angry look. His features twisted, and he pressed his mouth into a straight line.

She realized she sounded like an idiot, but she had no one to blame but herself. Finally, heat prickling her skin, she said, "Clint will specify."

Abruptly she turned on her heel and made her way down one of the aisles. She pretended to study the assortment of ropes hanging on one wall.

A few minutes later, minutes that seemed to span eternity, Clint walked over to her. "You ready?"

"Are you done?" she asked, countering his question.

"Uh-huh." Humor glinted in his brown eyes. "Of course, if you're not finished looking at these ropes, we can stay longer."

"No, I'm finished," she mumbled.

Her embarrassment eased as they headed for the door, and she realized her shoulder and neck muscles had tightened.

"We'll get that feed out to y'all tomorrow mornin' early," Earl said with a wave as they faced the windy outdoors.

"Earl's a good neighbor," Clint said, joining her in the truck's cab.

"Hmm, I suppose." She set the truck in motion. She flipped the switch for the heater, but only cold air brushed her legs. A chill crept up her spine. She stiffened and hoped the cab would warm up with a little time.

"He's a talker." Clint shifted in his seat and ran his hand down his thigh, drawing her attention to the hard muscles beneath the denim. "I, um, hope Earl didn't upset you none. What with his going on and on about your grandpa."

She shook her head. "No, he didn't. I'm fine."

But all that talk *had* bothered her.

She hadn't thought much about her grandfather over the years. She could barely remember the weekends she'd spent at the ranch as a small child. She hadn't been told about her grandmother's death until she was an adult. Now she had to face the fact that her grandparents had been flesh and blood. Guilt trickled through her until she corked the leak. Her grandfather had lived and died without much word from her. He'd loved her from the first. Had he been disappointed, saddened, when she didn't come to visit? She rolled her lips inward, fighting the guilt that honked at her conscience like an irritating New York taxi driver.

Finally, she confessed, "I didn't know him, my grandfather, very well. I haven't…hadn't seen him in years."

Clint didn't respond.

After a few minutes, she reached over and turned on the staticky radio, which received only AM stations. A twangy country-and-western song with a warbly male voice filled the cab with a tension-relieving, toe-tapping beat. Tamara's brow furrowed, and her grip tightened on the wheel. She switched stations, tuning in to some kind of slow, waltzy elevator music. Eventually her tension eased, the music acting like an elixir.

"Tammy Jo, huh?" Clint said, glancing over at her.

"What?" Her nerves stood on end.

"Oh, nothing, I was just saying it. It's a pretty name, rolls right off the tongue. Tammy Jo Lambert. Has a nice ring to it. Tammy—"

"It's Tamara, thank you."

"Ain't nothing to be ashamed of. Lots of folks around these parts have double names. Bobby Joe, Lou Ann, Betty Jean..." His voice drifted. "Tammy Jo's kind of friendly-sounding. Were you named after your grandpa? Old Joe, that is?"

She ground her teeth. She didn't want to feel a connection with her grandfather. She didn't want to sound friendly or chipper or like the girl next door. She wanted to make a sophisticated impression, and Tammy Jo didn't do that.

"I was not named after my grandfather. My name is Tamara Lambert. My grandfather gave me that—" she couldn't bring herself to say it "—nickname."

He stared at her, making her skittish, making her feel like a caged animal in a zoo, a novelty to be gawked at. Her venom never seemed to fire any temper in him. He remained calm and cool, as if he were a spectator, rather than a participant.

"So, you're a Texan," he said. "Born right here, huh? I would have never guessed."

"I should hope not."

"Not happy with your family background, I take it?"

"I'm a Texan by default only."

"What's that supposed to mean?" A defensive tone had deepened his voice.

She shook her head, not wanting to start a fight now. She didn't have the energy for it. She felt suddenly tired. She and Clint were too different. Oil and water never mixed. She didn't think there was any reason to force the issue any further. "It doesn't matter."

"Sure it does. Texans are proud of their state. It's God's

country. I haven't ever met anyone who wasn't proud to be—''

"Well, now you have." Tamara glanced over at him, and regretted her harsh words.

His brow furrowed. She'd hurt his Texas pride. He was proud of his state and his heritage. That pricked her conscience. But Texas had caused too much pain. Connecticut had brought relief from family pressures.

She realized then that she'd taken her own anger over hearing about her grandfather out on Clint. That had not been fair. He had his own memories of Old Joe, just as she had hers. She wanted to explain her reasons for not liking Texas or wanting to stay here—whether for her own assurance or for Clint, she wasn't sure.

"I didn't mean to tread on sacred ground." She shrugged. "Then again, maybe I did. But I didn't intend to insult you." She took a shallow breath. "I'm sure Texas is as fine a state as any. But it's just, well, I haven't lived here for a long time. My family moved to Connecticut when I was six. And I haven't been here on the ranch since then." A shudder rippled through her at the memory. "That's the last time I saw my grandparents." Her emotions tightened her throat.

"Why?" he asked.

"My father didn't get along with my grandfather. Old Joe was…set in his ways." That, she thought, said it nicely. "Anyway…" She glanced at him. The softness in his brown eyes touched her like a balm. She returned her gaze to the road. "Being a Texan, or really, my Texas accent, was—"

"*You* had a Texas accent?" His surprise made a grin spread across her face.

"Sure." She liked the fact that she'd surprised him. She didn't fit into the round hole he'd so obviously tried to put her in.

"You couldn't tell now, what with that Yankee accent." He exaggerated his own drawl. "Maybe I should call you Tex."

She gave him a wry smile, not wanting him to adopt a nickname, especially that one, because it seemed too personal, too intimate, and too much what she didn't want to be.

She ignored his comment and kept her tone light with "I could drawl with the best of them. Draw out one-syllable words into four. But my accent faded with time, as I was immersed in the New England culture." She shrugged. "So, now I sound like a Yankee. I no longer fit in here. And I certainly don't want to."

"Well, don't worry, Tex. You're welcome here. Yankee accent and all."

He'd called her Tex again. It should make her angry, she thought. But, for some reason, it didn't. At least it was better than "ma'am." Quickly she reminded herself that she didn't care if she was welcome here or not. She was leaving as soon as she could.

Chapter Three

"Ryan, get Mandy on the bus," Clint called to his nephew. He grabbed his hat off the peg by the door and settled it on his head. Chores were waiting. Cattle were hungry. Getting the kids up and ready, fed and dressed, put him behind schedule. All morning they'd bickered like magpies. He wondered why his father and brother had given up the sweet serenity of range work for the headache of families.

He opened the front door of the cottage house to step onto the porch, and nearly collided with his boss. His nerves already frayed like an unraveled rope, he stared down at Tamara. They stood only a few inches apart. Her light, airy scent fogged his brain for a moment. Her blue eyes looked as wide as a Texas summer sky.

"Morning, Tex," he managed, his voice thick. "Is there a problem?"

She held out a paintbrush. His gaze shifted downward, at the bristles, then to her hand, which was clenched around the paint-speckled handle, and finally up to her breasts. Full and round, perfect for the fit of a man's hand. His abdomen tightened with need. He hadn't had time for a woman since he inherited the kids. And he didn't have time now. And sure not with a Yankee. He jerked his gaze back to her face.

Irritation over his attraction to her stiffened his resolve. "Gonna paint the house, are you?"

"*You* are," she said, her jaw squared with determination. "The paint's being unloaded down by the barn right now."

They stood toe-to-toe, and she met his gaze. The tilt of her chin showed her confidence. It made him grin. She didn't know one damn thing about running a ranch.

"Gotta feed the cattle first. Then all that feed is arriving from Earl's. It's gotta be loaded in the barn." He squinted toward the hazy gray sky. "Before it decides to rain. If you wanna heft fifty-pound bags, then go ahead. I'll stay here and paint."

Her brows slanted into a frown. "*Then* you are going to paint. Right?"

He pushed the brim of his hat up with his thumb and squinted against the sun's glare. "Well, now—"

"Clint," she said, interrupting him, "I've been patient. But this is important. This place isn't likely to sell if it continues to look as run-down as it does."

He had no answer for her. He didn't much care if her ranch sold or not. That wasn't his job. His job was tending to the cattle. Couldn't she understand that?

Her stare turned frosty, the blue in her eyes icy. "That's it, isn't it?"

"What?"

"You don't want me to sell this place." She planted her fists on her hips. "You want to keep me trapped here."

"No, ma'am. I wouldn't say that. If you don't wanna stay here in Texas, then you might as well get on back east."

"Then why won't you do what I ask?"

He took a step toward her, and the hand that held the paint brush touched his abdomen. She held it firmly against him, without retreating. "Because, Miz Lambert, you don't know the first thing about running a ranch. If I was to do all you want me to do, then the cattle would go hungry or get sick and die.

"You don't seem to understand that the cattle mean as much profit as the ranch. Any rancher interested in buying the ranch is gonna be more interested in the herd and contours of the land than the damn houses.

"I'm doing my job. I'm a cowboy. Not a painter." Sidestepping around her, he tipped his hat. "I'll see you later. Time's a-wasting, and I have work to do."

Her blood boiled in her veins. She wheeled around and watched him saunter toward the barn, his shadow trailing after him at a lazy, no-need-to-hurry pace that matched his carefree attitude. Her anger never seemed to bother him; he always shrugged it off as easily as he would a jacket.

For some reason, she wanted to see him fire-eating mad. Maybe because she knew how to deal with that. Her father had a temper that rivaled dynamite. But not Clint. His easygoing personality rubbed her the wrong way.

She clenched her teeth and tried to think of something to say, something to convince him of the importance of painting this house. But she couldn't. Obviously, he was right. And she hated to be wrong.

With a puff of hot air toward her bangs, she decided that she had no choice. She would have to paint the house herself. After locating a rickety old wooden ladder, she leaned it up against the side of her grandparents' home. One step at a time, she hoisted herself up as she balanced the bucket of paint in one hand and the brush in the other. The ladder wobbled beneath her weight, and she glanced down at the ground, which seemed farther and farther away. Finally, she reached the top and set the bucket on the ladder's shelf.

After a while, she found a rhythm in stroking the weathered side of the house with her paintbrush. The clouds had dispersed, leaving a bright blue sky. The new white paint glistened in the sun as it shifted overhead from the easterly direction of morning to the western slant of afternoon. Eventually she shed her jacket and managed to splotch her clothes with dabs of paint. Her arm ached, and her back grew stiff from standing so long.

"You missed a spot." Clint's voice startled her.

Her nerves jumped. She glanced over her shoulder and glared down at him. He smiled at her, his mouth curving beneath the arch of his mustache. The ladder creaked. She felt herself tilt backward, and she threw her weight forward toward the ladder. She bobbled, frantically looking for a place to grab on to for support. Teetering, she felt herself fall. She saw the rooftop grow more and more distant.

Her heart pounded, and she squeezed her eyes shut. She braced herself for a hard impact with the ground.

With a thud and a groan, she hit something rock-hard, but she bounced as if she were floating in midair. Solid bands of iron held her against something warm and safe. She opened her eyes and stared into serious brown eyes flecked with concern.

"You okay, Tex?" he asked, holding her in his arms.

She nodded, unable to get a single word past her heart, which was jammed in her throat. She noticed then that her arm was slung over his shoulder, and she felt his hard muscles beneath her palm. His chest was solid against her side. His heat singed her. His breath warmed her ear.

Her heart fluttered. An odd sensation rippled through her. She felt as if she belonged there, in his arms. It unnerved her.

Slowly he bent his knees and tilted forward. As he set

her feet on the ground, his face came close to her breast. She held her breath. Her knees dipped, and she clung to him. He straightened, and his hands bracketed her waist. Blistering shocks of awareness ignited all along her body. She felt the heat of his gaze on her. Her breath caught in her chest.

Gritting her teeth, she stepped away from him and hoped her legs wouldn't collapse beneath her. She managed to find her own footing, then finally glanced up at him. His face had hardened like granite, with deep grooves running lengthwise down his cheeks. His mouth was straight as an arrow, softened only by the curve of his mustache.

"Thanks," she managed, her voice breathless.

"My pleasure, Tamara." Her name rolled off his tongue and sent a hot surge of awareness through her. It was the first time he'd called her that, not "ma'am" or "Miz Lambert" or "Tex" or the dreaded "Tammy Jo." And she liked the way he said it, in his slow, Texas drawl.

She decided then that she preferred it when he called her "ma'am." It was infinitely safer. After all, he wasn't her type. He was a cowboy with his boots firmly planted in traditions that contradicted hers. He was a family man. She was a loner. She liked her independence. It would be too easy to depend on a man like Clint Morgan.

He grinned. "You said when you hired me that a foreman had to do a lot of different things around the ranch, but I never imagined I'd have to catch you. Or hold you. Or—"

He leaned closer. Her gaze dropped to his mouth. He stared into her eyes. His hot breath fanned her face. She licked her lips. God, she was thinking about kissing him. Had she lost her mind? A hot blush set fire to her cheeks, and she shifted away from him.

"Me either." She forced the words through her tight throat and broke the spell between them.

He gave her a lazy smile that curled her insides, then glanced up at the ladder. "Least the paint didn't fall."

Relieved she hadn't kissed him—or the other way around—she followed his gaze to the bucket perched on the top of the ladder. "That would have been a huge mess."

"You sound almost disappointed."

"I'm not," she said defensively.

He rubbed his jaw. The bristles rasped across his palm, and the sound tickled her insides with an odd tingle.

Her gaze narrowed as she tried to focus her attention on the house, rather than on Clint. "You said I missed a spot. Where?"

He stepped toward her, closing the gap between them and making it harder for her to draw a deep breath. She smelled his powerful scent. Man and leather and outdoors. Sunshine and heat. She tried to concentrate on the paint fumes. But he overwhelmed her with his masculinity, and made her light-headed.

So she focused on the fact that they were completely incompatible. She was a city girl who liked Macy's and dinner before going to the theater. He was a *cowboy*.

Enough said about that.

"Here's where you missed a spot." With his forefinger, he touched the tip of her nose.

Confusion blurred her thoughts. She blinked and looked straight into his deep brown eyes.

"You painted yourself as much as the house." He chuckled, his gaze roaming over her with the practiced ease of a lover's touch.

A shiver rippled through her. "Oh, I must look a mess."

"Nope," he drawled. "You look kinda cute."

Cute! Her hands clenched. If she'd wanted to be considered cute, then she might as well have answered to Tammy Jo. Or, for that matter, Tex.

"Of course," he continued, "I liked you with mud splattered on your..." His voice faded, and his facial features tightened. "Uh, here." He bent and retrieved her paintbrush, which had fallen in the dry, brittle grass. Bits of shriveled blades clung to the wet paint. "Why don't you stay off the ladder for a while? Paint down below. I'll take care of the eaves and the higher spots."

"You'll help me?"

He nodded and removed his hat. "Guess I'll have to."

His agreement flustered her. Still, she gave him her best smile of appreciation.

Her smile made the lowly task of painting the house bearable, even worth it. Clint knew he should paint and keep his mind off Tamara. But after holding her in his arms, feeling her body pressed tight to his, he found his senses tuned to her every movement, her soft, alluring scent, her sweet smile.

And her paint-freckled face made her look vulnerable and friendly and too damn appealing.

He knew he was in trouble by the time he finished painting the eaves. The afternoon felt as hot as his desire. Without a word, he washed out the brushes and put away the leftover cans of paint. He needed to get far away from Tamara.

As he walked toward the barn for escape, he heard a soft chuckle from behind him. He turned.

"Forget something, cowboy?" Tamara twirled his Stetson around her index finger.

Retracing his steps, he plowed his fingers through his hair.

"Did the paint job age you?" she asked.

No, he thought, hanging around her had. "What do you mean?"

She reached out and fingered a lock of his hair. A wave

of desire, hot and urgent and fierce, swept over him. He should have backed away, but he couldn't force his feet to move.

"You grew a few gray hairs this afternoon." Again she laughed. "The paint," she explained. "Seems I'm not the only one who missed the house with the brush."

Finally, catching on to her joke, he managed a smile. "Bet it doesn't look as cute on me."

She tilted her head. "Makes you look very distinguished."

Her husky tone knotted his insides.

"Would you like a glass of iced tea, or lemonade, or something?" she asked, staring up at him with those fathomless blue eyes.

"Uh...I've got a few more chores to do at the barn." He stepped away, knowing he needed more distance.

"Oh, come on. You deserve at least a beer."

That invitation undermined his better judgement. How could he turn that down? His throat felt as dry as the desert. What harm could a quick beer cause? He wouldn't have to talk to her. He'd just drink a beer and then get on with his chores. He might even take the beer with him to the barn.

"Okay," he finally agreed.

A few moments later, he found himself on the porch, sitting in the swing, sipping an ice-cold beer. Tamara sat next to him. A little too close for his comfort.

Uneasy with the silence, he asked, "So what's your hurry about getting back east? I mean, you must have some great job."

"I like it." Her blue gaze seemed distant, almost reflective.

"Or is it a boyfriend or something that's making you want to get back?" His gaze shifted to his beer bottle. Now why'd he asked that?

"No," she said quickly.

"Your family want you back home?"

"I don't live with my folks. We're not very close. I do my own thing. As they've always done theirs. I was raised to be independent."

He could well believe that. "So you got some high-powered executive job, then?"

She glanced away, then back at him with a slight but perceptible lift to her chin. "I manage a bookstore."

Surprised, he gazed at her, noticing how her eyes sparkled. "Yeah? What kind of books?"

"All kinds. Fiction, biographies, self-help—"

"Any history books?" he asked, his interest piqued.

"Sure."

"I bet the new bookstore in Georgetown has more in the way of Texas history."

"Probably." She studied him for a moment, and he felt restless suddenly. "You like history?"

He nodded. "Texas, mostly. You know, stuff on the Alamo or the Texas Revolution. But I also like anything on the old West."

"Really?" Her eyes widened with surprise.

"You probably thought I couldn't read, huh?"

"No," she said, quickly, defensively. "I just… Well, it surprised me. I guess I figured you wouldn't have much time to read." Her cheeks grew pink. "What I meant to say was that you seem like a very active man, not inclined to sit around and…" She cut her eyes toward him, her chin tilting down shyly. "I'm not explaining myself very well."

"Don't worry about it. I'm not surprised you had a few preconceived notions about a cowboy. Most people stereotype us. That's okay. Besides, I had you pegged as a typical Yankee."

"You did?" The corner of her mouth lifted enticingly. "I'm not typical, then?"

"Not one bit." He tore his gaze from her and swigged his beer.

She cleared her throat and shifted in her seat, rocking the swing. "So, when do you find time to read about history?"

"Oh, not so much anymore. When I rode the range, I had time at night, around the campfire. When I wasn't looking after the herd."

"Sounds romantic, out on some prairie beside a roaring fire."

"Mostly it was cold in winter and hot in summer. Insects and snakes took away most of the romance."

"But you loved it," she said smiling. "I can tell."

"Yeah. I loved it." He missed it now. He missed the wind in the trees, the sun on his back, the sight of mountains in the distance. But that life was over.

He took another pull on his beer and felt Tamara's gaze on him. The easy conversation made him nervous. He felt more comfortable when they argued than he did now. This connection forming between them, he feared, was dangerous.

"So, how come you hate Texas?" he asked, hoping to spark anger in her.

She bristled. "I don't hate Texas. I just prefer to live back east, where I was raised."

"Didn't you ever come visit your grandparents?"

"Yes." The word sounded clipped.

"But not in a long while?"

"That's right." She crossed her arms over her chest and cradled her beer between her thighs.

Clint's throat constricted. He pressed his point. "Okay, it's this ranch, then, that you hate."

Her mouth thinned. "I wouldn't say that." She ducked her head. "But I don't have fond memories of visiting here."

"How come?"

She shrugged. "My father didn't get along with my grandfather. They argued constantly."

The concept seemed foreign to Clint. He'd been close to his family, which made the separation by death more acutely painful.

Tamara glanced at him then. "They were different men. I know you liked my grandfather. It's not that I don't...didn't. But I knew a different side of him."

"What's that?"

"He was stubborn. Set in his ways. And more often than not, his way was right and anything that differed from that was wrong. Which happened to be my father's ideas on life, too."

Clint downed the rest of his beer. It was time to leave, but he couldn't make himself. He wanted to hear more. The pain in her eyes held him captive.

She clasped her hands together. "My grandfather was content with this place." She glanced out at the ranch. He guessed she only saw what was wrong—weeds, broken fence posts and weathered barns—not the beauty in the far-reaching sky and fertile grassy plains. "Barely making a living here. Living hand-to-mouth. But my father wanted more. My father wanted to make something of himself. And he did."

"Is that what you think?" he asked, narrowing his gaze on her. "That your grandfather was a nobody because he didn't accomplish all your father thought he should?"

She stared at her hands. "I think there's more to life than living on a ranch."

"Yeah, I do, too." This proved their differences. "But don't think your grandfather was a failure. He made a good living. He provided for his family. He had a solid reputation as a good rancher." He saw the disbelief in her eyes. "He was a good man. A fine neighbor. He touched a lot of lives. Even isolated way out here. He was admired by many.''

But he knew she didn't believe him. Something strange and disappointing opened inside him.

Saturday arrived, and with it the real threat of buyers. In the shade of the barn, Clint sat on his boot heels, his hat squared low over his brow. Even in early November, the sun could bake the dry, rocky ground as if it were a hot summer day. Fall in the hill country tended to be as fickle as a teenage girl. He squinted against the sun's rays, bouncing off the whiteness of the newly painted cottage house. Why couldn't it be raining? An early snowfall would even be welcome, he thought. Anything to make the ranch unwelcoming to strangers.

A dose of guilt showed him that maybe Tamara had been right. He didn't want her to sell the ranch. Not for her to stay here. Because that would never happen. She didn't fit in here. Her comments about her grandfather made Clint feel defensive about Old Joe. Part of him wanted to show her what a wonderful man he'd been. Part of him wanted her to continue believing what she did, so she'd pack up and leave.

Still, he didn't want her to sell out, because if she did he'd lose his job. It was selfish. But honest.

He stared across the yard, and his gut twisted. A middle-aged couple, the man tall and lanky as a string bean and the woman plump as a ripe tomato, wandered about the property. Barbara Cooper, the real estate agent, walked a few steps ahead of them, giving them the grand tour.

Tension coiled inside Clint. What would he do if the ranch sold this week? This month? It wasn't so much a question of *if* the ranch would sell as *when*. He had to figure out where he'd take the kids. He had to find something permanent. Something secure.

The couple walked toward him, and Clint rose to his full height. Tamara Lambert, no matter what he thought of her, paid his check. He wouldn't do anything to sabotage her efforts to sell her grandfather's ranch.

"This is the foreman," Miss Cooper said, "Clint Morgan. He's a well-respected cowboy. Grew up right here in Georgetown, and he's ranched all over the country."

"Well, howdy." The gentleman shook Clint's hand. "Name's Abbott. Henry Abbott, and my wife, Edna." Mrs. Abbott smiled, and Clint nodded in her direction.

"Over here…" Miss Cooper edged toward the barn, obviously not willing to linger in one place for long, but she stopped when the Abbotts seemed content to pass the time of day in the shade.

Henry Abbott swiped the sweat off his brow and combed his thinning gray hair back in place. "Nice ranch you have here."

"Yes, sir." Clint shifted his weight to his other foot. His gaze cut toward Tamara, who stood on the front porch of her house. He knew how much she wanted to sell this place, and he could imagine her nerves dancing the jitterbug while she awaited the Abbotts' decision.

After a moment's hesitation, she descended the steps and headed toward the barn. She had an easy stroll, one Clint realized matched his own long stride. Her hips rolled in a motion that drew his attention.

"You buildin' that corral over there?" Abbott asked.

Clint shifted his attention back to the potential buyer and crossed his arms over his chest. "Uh, yes, sir—just about to finish it."

The man nodded. "Hard work diggin' those postholes. Enough to break a man's back. I helped my father do that type of work when I was a youngster."

"It can be tough," Clint agreed. It wasn't his favorite chore, but nothing could compare to riding the range, looping a rope around a heifer and guiding her back to the herd. Still, that life was over, and his new one, which meant digging postholes, mucking out the stalls in the barn and painting houses, had begun. "It's not so bad if you're used to it, I suppose."

"Is everything all right?" Tamara asked as she approached. Her blue eyes clouded as she looked from the real estate agent to the Abbotts to Clint.

"It's awful warm today," Abbott replied. "Just thought we'd lollygag in the shade for a bit and chat with your foreman."

"I see." Tamara managed a terse smile, then worried her bottom lip between her teeth.

The tension pulled the minutes out like taffy at the state fair. A fly whizzed by Clint's ear. A soft breeze stirred the air and carried the distant sound of a calf bawling. Henry Abbott pulled his pipe out of his pocket, tapped it on his boot heel and filled the bowl with an aromatic tobacco. He struck the match, and the flame flared. Slowly a stream of smoke rose. The wind caught it and carried it away in a warm breath.

"How many cows you got?" Henry Abbott broke the silence.

"Around three hundred, I think," Clint said.

Abbott's brow wrinkled. "Don't most ranchers keep notes on such as that?"

Clint hooked his thumbs in his belt loops. "That depends on the ranch. Miz Lambert's granddaddy was pretty sick before he passed on, and, well, things might have slacked off a bit."

"I see." Abbott rubbed his jaw with his thumb. "That's a shame. I'm sorry, ma'am, I didn't realize."

"It's okay." She gave a weak smile.

"Joe Lambert's reputation for fine beef reaches beyond this county, all the way to Austin," Abbott said.

"Well, the beeves are still the same good quality," Clint added.

"How much yield in hay do you get each year?" Abbott asked, his gaze settling on the tractor.

"About six or seven hundred bales, I'd say."

"That much?"

"Yes, sir. There's good pastureland here on the outskirts of the hill country. We have a few rocks and cacti, but nothin' that old tractor can't handle. If you get three or four good cuttings, that ought to carry you through the winter.

"We might have to buy some hay come January, seein' that Miz Lambert's granddaddy didn't get around to the third cutting this summer."

"Sounds expensive," Abbott said.

"Can be. Depends on if there was enough rain throughout the summer for others trying to sell hay."

Abbott shook his head. "Sounds like lots of upkeep."

"There's always something needs fixin'," Clint agreed.

"You could hire Clint," Tamara suggested.

Surprised by her statement, Clint glanced at her.

The older man nodded. "That's usually a pretty hefty expense. No offense, son, but I figure if I'm gonna own a ranch, then I oughta be able to do the work myself."

"No shame in that." Clint swallowed any hope he'd entertained about continuing on if the Abbotts bought the place. "You can hire high school boys during hay season for cheap labor. Old Joe hired me—" Clint rubbed his jaw, remembering "—when I was sixteen years old. Taught me more than I wanted to know about hay and sweat and heat that summer."

Abbott nodded. "Boy, I remember sweatin' like that when I was a youngster."

Mrs. Abbott placed her hand on her husband's arm. "That could be bad for your health."

The older gentleman waved his arm. "The barns, corrals,

cattle… It's a lot to maintain. And we're not young whip-persnappers anymore.''

Clint nodded. ''It's not something to be taken lightly….''

''Clint!'' Tamara broke in. ''Didn't you have work out in the south pasture to do? Weren't you going to count cows or something?'' Her tone was like a barb in his saddle.

His gaze bore into her. She made him feel like an out-of-line schoolkid. He detected a thread of panic in her voice, but her eyes looked ice-cold. Without hesitation, he nodded. ''Yes'm.'' He tipped the brim of his hat to the Abbotts and headed toward the pickup. ''Have a nice tour, folks.''

Clint didn't know what had riled Tamara, and he re-played the conversation in his mind, trying to figure out what he could have said. Maybe she was afraid of what he might say. Not that he would say anything to hurt the sale of the ranch. Not that there was much to say. From Clint's vantage point, this place was all a man could dream of. Already, after a week of working the land and cattle, his affection had been yoked to the Bar L Ranch.

He didn't want to ever have to leave. But he knew he would. And probably soon.

A squeal like a stuck pig made Clint flinch. He caught sight of Mandy a few yards from the truck. She snorted and pawed the ground, pointing her fingers out from her temples like a bull. She charged Ryan, who turned her aside with a hand to her head. A nearby cow shied away. The rest of the cattle watched, ears pricked, bodies tense.

''Whoa!'' Clint said. ''Do y'all want to start a stampede with all that racket? Get up here in the truck.''

''Could we really scare the cows?'' Mandy skipped to-ward the truck, and Ryan followed at his own pace.

''Yep,'' Clint answered, then gave her a quick smile.

"No harm done. You just have to be careful. These old cows aren't used to too many visitors. Especially little kids. They probably haven't seen a horse in years. Only Mr. Lambert and this old pickup when he'd come to feed 'em. These cows are skittish."

Shaking his head, he spotted an old cow with bulging sides. It wouldn't be long before she delivered. She walked with the stiffness of age, and he decided to cut her out of the herd. That way, he could put her up in the barn so he could watch her progress.

"Hey, look!" Mandy pointed behind Clint.

Startled, he glanced over his shoulder and saw Tamara astride Old Red, Mr. Lambert's sorrel gelding. He squinted against the sun. Her silhouette stood out plain against the brow of the hill. From the confident squaring of her shoulders and the relaxed position of her hands as they held the reins, he knew she was an experienced rider. Without a visible signal from her, the horse moved forward, picking its way down the rocky slope.

As the horse and rider reached the bottom, they sprang into a gallop. Tamara posted, her legs acting like springs. Clint's mouth quirked in a smile. She was even a Yankee on horseback, riding English-style. Her mahogany hair streamed behind her and lapped against her shoulders. The rocking movement had an erotic effect on Clint, and his gut tightened. His throat became like the dry, parched ground, and he swallowed hard.

In self-defense, he ticked off the reasons he should stay clear of Tamara, enumerating them in his head. He had no time for romance, no inclination, no need. She was a Yankee, for God's sake! And she was ready to leave Texas as quick as she had come. That sobered his desire for her like a cup of his hottest, blackest range coffee.

A calf bawled, and its mother's bellowing followed. The old pregnant cow bolted. She swerved in time to miss

Mandy. The herd scattered. Clint leaped to the ground and swung his niece into the bed of the truck. Ryan jumped in after her. The thunder of hooves echoed in Clint's head. Anger thrummed inside him.

Tamara rode straight for him, then reined in her mount abruptly beside the truck. The gelding's nostrils flared. Clint grabbed the horse's halter and glared up at Tamara. Her eyes flashed like blue fire. She seemed oblivious of the chaos as the cattle ran for the farthest corners of the ranch.

"I can't believe you!" Heat saturated her words.

"Excuse me?" The dust choked him. "What about you?"

She ignored his accusation. "Why did you try to sabotage the sale of this ranch?"

He took a deep, cleansing breath and released his own temper. "You caused a stampede. And my niece and nephew were almost trampled."

Her gaze swerved toward the truck behind him. Her features softened into concern. "What happened?"

He tightened his grip on the horse's halter and tried to strangle his temper. "You came over that hill hell-bent for I don't know what. These old cows haven't seen a horse in years. It scared them out of a year's worth of hay.

"They took off for safety. Mandy and Ryan could have been…" He let the unspoken phrase complete his sentence with a deathlike silence. "What the hell did you think you were doing?"

"I—I wanted to talk to you." Every line of her body seemed to tremble as her anger faltered.

"About what?"

"What you said to Mr. Abbott."

The muscles in his neck and shoulders contracted like a vise. "What did I say that got you so hot under the collar?"

"Well—" the fire had left her eyes "—you were playing

right into his excuses that he lined up for not buying the ranch.''

He clamped his jaws shut in frustration. ''A man can't change another one's mind in that short of a period of time.''

She squared her shoulders and squinted at him. ''What right is it of yours to tell a potential buyer what needs to be fixed?''

''He asked me a question, and I answered it. With the truth. That's all. He could see that plain as day himself.'' His own gaze narrowed, reflecting his aggravation. ''Were you trying to hide the truth?''

''No, but...'' She stammered. Her mount shifted restlessly beneath her. ''You just don't want me to sell.''

''That didn't have anything to do with what I said back there. The man asked questions. What did you want me to say?''

''Nothing. You shouldn't have been talking to him in the first place.''

''Miss Cooper introduced us.''

''Just to be polite,'' she countered.

''Mr. Abbott wanted to talk to me, man to man. I answered his questions honestly. I have no regrets about that.'' He faltered for a moment, but couldn't keep from defending himself. ''And if you want to know the truth of the matter...'' He took a step toward her. His stomach was inches from her knee. ''...I think you're afraid, Tex.''

He let the nickname grate on her nerves like her accent did him. She didn't look like a Tex or a Tammy Jo at the moment. She wore tight-fitting riding pants, the sissy kind that Yankees used. But he couldn't deny that they showed off her sleek figure. Still, he decided he liked her a lot better in jeans, with mud all over her butt or paint on her nose. Then she'd looked like a Tammy Jo, friendly and unpretentious.

Her chin jutted forward with indignation as she took his bait. "Afraid of what?"

"That you're not going to sell this place. Frightened out of your wits that you're going to be stuck here. In Texas. Which might not be a bad idea." He'd said enough. Too much.

His gaze scanned the horizon, and he saw that a few cows had stopped their flight. At least the crisis was over, but there was no telling what damage had been done. No matter what, at least Mandy and Ryan were safe in the bed of the truck.

"You're right, though—" he lowered his voice "—I don't want you to sell. Maybe that's selfish, maybe that's loco.

"When a man works as hard as your grandfather worked to build this place into what it is, then he usually doesn't want it sold before his memory's cold. So, yeah, I'd like to see you make a go of it here. You might like Texas if you were to give it a fair shot. You are a Texan, whether you want to admit it or not. But get this straight—" he poked her boot-covered calf with his forefinger "—I did not sabotage your sale. No matter what I want, no matter how it affects me, I would never do that."

They stared at each other for a full minute, the air sizzling between them like bacon frying in a cast-iron skillet. Realizing that he'd said too much, and that he'd raised his voice to his boss, he shook his head and cursed himself for being a fool. He jammed his hands into his back pockets and waited for her to speak. Waited for her to fire him.

She blinked, her mouth working silently before she finally said, "I don't like Texas. I never have, and I never will. And I like cowboys even less." Her meaning jabbed at him like a red hot poker. "I'm not staying here, so get that through your thick skull, cowboy. I'm going to sell the Bar L Ranch. And that's final."

Chapter Four

Tamara's body trembled, anger and embarrassment rippling through her. She shut her mouth before she could say anything else. Damn Clint Morgan for ruining this sale for her. Henry Abbott had been interested. She'd been sure of it. Then, after a few minutes with Clint, Abbott had decided the ranch required too much work. More work than he was willing to do once he retired. Damn.

She stared at Clint, her anger simmering, spritzed out of its burning rage by his rebuke that had hit too close to its mark. She ought to fire him. But she couldn't. She hated to admit it, but she needed him. At least until the ranch sold.

Clint met her stare with a burning intensity, his eyes glowing like embers. The furrow in his brow told her his anger matched hers, but he held it in check. She'd accused him of undermining her plans, and she realized then that a man such as Clint wouldn't tolerate his honor being attacked.

The children were watching them. Mandy's eyes were

wide. Ryan was smirking, as if it were all a show for his teenage amusement.

"Get off your horse," Clint said, his voice resonating in her own chest.

She jerked the reins, and the horse tossed its head. Indignant, she bristled. She'd wondered what would push Clint to get angry, and now she was sorry she'd been the one to push the wrong button. "What for?"

Clint's dark eyes blazed. His nostrils flared. A warning that she'd pushed him too far sounded in her brain. She drew in a thin stream of air.

"I'm going to round up the herd that you scattered hither and yon. You could have run the cows through a fence. A calf could have been injured or killed. Hell, they could have turned this truck over in their fright. I've got to go see what damage has been done. And fix it. That's my job. And I want to use your horse."

She had no comeback, nothing to answer his accusations with. The truth of his words stamped guilt on her heart. She stared at his niece and nephew and felt remorseful that she'd put them in danger. Her face burned beneath Clint's steady gaze.

"Then," he continued, not letting up, "I'm going to cut out one of the older cows and move her down to the barn so I can watch her. If she hasn't calved because of this fright."

"For what?" She stumbled over the words.

"To be sure she doesn't have any problems when she drops her calf. Which probably won't be too long now."

Properly put in her place, Tamara regretted her recklessness. She tried to excuse her behavior with all the reasons she'd wanted to confront Clint, but still, she knew it had been dangerous and stupid. And it might have been deadly to his niece and nephew.

"I'm sorry," she said. "I..." Explanations, she realized,

would be meaningless words to Clint, and would never appease his anger. He was a man of action, who only valued the actions of others. "I'll take your niece and nephew back to the house and make dinner."

He nodded, accepting her implied apology. "I'd appreciate that."

She dismounted, her shoulder brushing against his chest as she slid to the ground.

He glared at her English saddle. "I don't need this contraption."

With stiff motions, as if he were trying to contain his anger, he unhitched the girth and tossed her fine leather saddle in the back of the pickup as if it were a scrap of garbage. Holding the reins with one hand, he swung himself onto the horse's bare back, his spurs jangling menacingly.

Immediately, his body seemed to relax. He tugged on the reins, then wheeled the gelding back to face Tamara. His mouth worked, as if he were struggling with something he needed to say. "I was out of line. I shouldn't have said what I did."

"Yes, you should have. You were doing your job. You're the ranch foreman. You were trying to protect the cattle I placed in your care. And, more importantly, your kids. I was in the wrong. I'll be more careful next time. I promise."

He nodded and rode away.

Tamara opened the oven and checked the pizzas. The warmth flowed over her. Yellow cheese bubbled on top of the pizzas, and the warm, spicy aromas of oregano and garlic wafted toward her. She reached for the hot pads.

A knock sounded at the door, and Mandy lunged for it. Tamara glanced up just as Clint stepped inside, his boots scuffing the wood floor as her grandfather's once had. His skin glistened with sweat, and his shirt stuck to his torso, outlining his defined muscles. A shock of awareness rocked through her as his bronze gaze scanned the room and settled on her.

"Everything okay?" she asked.

"Yeah."

"Any trouble?"

"Not as much as there could have been. Had to mend a couple of fences. But all the cattle are accounted for."

She breathed a sigh of relief. "Good. Thanks for taking care of everything."

"That's my job. But thanks for watching the kids."

"My pleasure."

The truce felt awkward to Tamara, as if an undercurrent of something were pulling at each of them. Suddenly self-conscious, Tamara broke eye contact and pulled a pizza out of the oven. She wore her grandmother's hot pads on her hands, and her jeans were splotched with flour. She was her grandmother reincarnated. She could imagine her hair turning a dull shade of gray and her stomach rounding from too many church bake sales. The coziness and warmth she'd felt a few minutes ago as she enjoyed getting to know his niece and nephew evaporated like morning dew. Once, a long time ago, when she was a child, she would have given anything to have a family scene such as this. But no more.

She pictured herself chained to a stove, her hips widening from too much gravy and her nails worn short from washing dishes, dusting furniture and cleaning commodes. She had a flash of Clint coming in the door, saying, "I'm home, darlin'," in his thick Texas drawl. He would grab her, kiss her and...

That wasn't what she wanted—being stuck here on a ranch in Texas like her grandparents, without a life. She closed the door on those thoughts and locked it.

Things had changed. She'd changed. She'd learned to

make her own family, her own friends. And this wasn't her family, her children, or her husband. She'd learned to rely on herself. Because that was all she had.

"Pizza's ready," she called. Both kids ran for the kitchen. Chair legs scraped the floor in their haste.

"Come on, Uncle Clint," Mandy said.

"Is there enough?" he asked. "I can grab a bite at the cottage house. We have plenty."

"No, no," Tamara said.

He peered at her from beneath the brim of his hat, and her nerves tightened.

"There's plenty." She raced through the red light in her mind that warned her of the danger of spending too much time with Clint. What else could she do? He deserved a good meal, after what she'd put him through today. "Come on and sit down."

She moved away from him, backing away from the magnetic pull of his gaze. She hooked a loose strand of hair behind her ear and offered as pleasant a smile as she could, under the circumstances. "It'll be a nice change for you."

He raised an eyebrow to her statement.

Catching her fumble, she explained, "Mandy told me that you only...well, that you could really cook some mouth-watering corn bread and spicy pinto beans."

"Ah." He grinned back at her.

Her stomach flip-flopped.

His smile beamed like a searchlight, piercing her resolve to ignore her attraction to him. He removed his cowboy hat, plopping it on the spindle-backed chair, and plowed his fingers through his unruly dark hair. A shock of hair fell across his forehead, and the overhead light gleamed in the thick waves. His hat band had left a crease around his head and made the ends of his hair curl along his nape.

He settled into a chair at one end of the table, stretching his long legs out in front of him. Her gaze followed the length of him, down his jeans to his worn boots. He clasped his hands across his middle. His forearms bulged, and the wisps of dark hair curling across his skin accented his tan. Her pulse quickened.

"I see my niece and nephew have been complaining," he joked.

Aware that she was being watched, she focused on slicing the pizzas. Her fingers felt clumsy. "I wouldn't say that exactly."

"Griping? Grumbling?" he offered, his smile still intact.

"More like—very appreciative of my home cooking. Which speaks volumes."

His appreciative gaze warmed her down to her toes. "I can't wait to try it, then, Tex."

She hated that nickname. She hated what it insinuated even more. In a conspiratorial tone, she whispered, "I'm not that good, cowboy."

"I wouldn't be so sure about that." His voice sounded like a low growl.

His lips uncurled. His mustache balanced the full curve of his lower lip. A burning heat filled his eyes. She swallowed hard, her face blazing with embarrassment. Her ears roared with the rush of blood pounding through her veins. A dizzying current raced through her, and she gripped the counter to steady herself.

Awareness flared between them, the air sizzling with a desire Tamara couldn't explain or deny. From his look, he wanted her. And she wanted him. Crazy as it seemed, it was the truth. In the same instant she understood that, she also knew there could never be anything between them. They were different. Not just in the obvious accents and accessories. They walked different paths. His remained here. In Texas. Hers took her back east. Home.

Turning her back on her desire and on Clint, she opened the refrigerator and found the salad dressing. She helped the children fill their plates with steaming cheesy slices, then sat across the table from him. She avoided his unnerving gaze, not allowing herself to react to him, as a woman to a man.

"This is yummy," the little girl said. Mandy licked the cheese off the top of her pizza slice, but left the crust on her plate.

"I'm glad you like it." Tamara chuckled at how the children gobbled their helpings of salad and most of the two pizzas. She watched them, amazed, because she knew she wasn't Julia Child.

"Mama used to make pizza and s'ghetti for us." The tone of the little girl's voice tugged at Tamara. "She died."

"Shut up," Ryan said.

"Ryan." Clint's voice brooked no argument.

"Well, she did." Mandy propped her hands on her hips.

"So did Dad. You don't gotta tell everybody." Anger filled Ryan's blue eyes.

Mandy stared at her plate.

Tamara's heart ached for the two orphaned children, who had stopped chewing, as if a moment of respect was required. Clint grabbed another piece of pizza, his movements choppy, his gaze downcast. Tamara swallowed the lump that had formed in her throat. What could she say now to lift the heavy silence?

"I'm sorry," she said, regretful that these children had faced death at such a young age.

Ryan shrugged. "It wasn't your fault. Some drunk driver ran into them on the highway. He's in jail."

"Mama and Daddy went to heaven," Mandy said, her sweet voice piercing the last vestiges of Tamara's control.

She blinked back tears. She wanted to hug the little girl to her, tell her it would be all right. But would it? Sadness ripped open her heart. She knew what it was like not to have parents. Not that her own parents had died. They just hadn't been around much. It hurt. And that pain never went away. But she was stronger for it. She wrapped her independence around the wound in her soul. And then she understood Ryan's brooding rage.

Reaching out, Tamara brushed back a lock of Mandy's fine blond hair off her forehead. This precious little girl had lost both of her parents in a single blow. Tamara's loss had been more gradual, and she couldn't imagine how anyone so small, so innocent, could comprehend the situation, much less cope.

She struggled to find a lighter topic, to restore the pleasant mood from earlier, to regain her own equilibrium. But how did she jump from their parents' deaths to MTV or Barbie dolls? She struggled with her tangled thoughts and surging emotions, trying to find a ray of hope in her clouded spirit.

"I'm gonna be a Pilgrim." Mandy's face lifted with a smile.

"You are?" Tamara automatically responded. "Where?"

"At school."

"Her kindergarten class is doing a program for Thanksgiving," Clint explained.

Mandy nodded. "And we're gonna sing and have pumpkin pie and corn on the cob and turkey and mashed potatoes and gravy."

"Pilgrims didn't eat mashed potatoes and gravy," Ryan said.

"Did too." Mandy's jaw squared with determination.

"Mandy's got to have a costume." Clint frowned, as if thinking to himself. "I completely forgot about that."

"I wanna be a boy Pilgrim," she piped in.

Tamara stared at the little girl who looked as determined as a football linebacker about to tackle the quarterback. "Why?"

"'Cause boys have more fun. All the girls back then had to cook and clean. The boys gotta fight and hunt and...everything.''

Tamara laughed. "How about if I help you make a costume?"

Her gaze sought Clint's. He stared at her for a moment, a wariness creeping into the brown depths of his eyes. She wanted to help him. Without a moment's thought about how she would even make a costume, she knew she wanted to try. For Mandy. For Clint.

"I couldn't let you do that," he said.

"Why?"

"Because...well, you're my boss. You have better things to do."

"You're a cowboy," she answered, "and I had you painting the house."

He grinned at that. "You got me with that one. But I still don't think it's right."

"What were you planning to do for a costume?" she challenged.

He shrugged. "I don't have a clue."

"All right, then, you have to let me help." She met his smile with one of her own. A warmth spread through her limbs. She felt good helping this young child, and this single parent struggling to keep this family together. "We'll make you a boy Pilgrim outfit, Mandy, with a stovepipe hat and corncob pipe and big buckles for your shoes."

"All right!" Mandy's eyes sparkled.

Clint glanced from his niece to Tamara. "You're sure about this?"

"Positive." She grinned.

"I really appreciate it," Clint said. "Thanks. And thanks for dinner, too. I know the kids enjoyed it. Something different from the usual." He gave her a wink that warmed her heart.

* * *

"Can Tamara read me a story?" Mandy asked.

Clint's heart contracted. He stood at the door, ready to herd his family back to the cottage house and get out of his boss's way. He'd grown used to reading Mandy bedtime stories himself. When he'd first taken custody of his niece and nephew, he'd felt awkward reading Dr. Seuss, but then he'd realized it was a fun way to learn about this little girl. Her inquisitive nature surprised, frustrated and amazed him. Now he felt territorial about his quiet time with her.

"No, darlin', it's getting late." Clint picked Mandy up in his arms. "Miz Lambert's probably tired of us by now."

"Not at all," Tamara said.

"See!" Mandy squealed.

Clint gritted his teeth. His niece probably missed a female influence in her life. He didn't fill her mother's shoes very well. But could he really impose like that on his boss? "I don't want to be a bother to you."

Tamara smiled. "I really don't mind."

How could he tell her no? How could he explain that it was his job? How could he refuse his niece and her wide, blue eyes? Relenting, he said, "Well, that would be awful nice."

A few minutes later, in the cottage house, Mandy and Tamara entered the little girl's bedroom. Feeling left out, Clint remained right outside the door, which stood ajar. Ryan had gone to his own room, and Clint waited, listening to Mandy and Tamara. He shouldn't eavesdrop, he reasoned, but a tightness in his chest and an emotion he couldn't name wouldn't let his feet budge from their position.

Peeking through the crack in the door opening, he watched Tamara sit on the edge of Mandy's bed. It was the exact spot where he usually sat and read to his niece. Frowning, he peered closer.

"What do you want me to read?" Tamara asked.

"The lost-kitty story." Mandy crawled into bed and slipped her feet beneath the covers. Clint usually folded the sheet and blanket back for her. "That one on top there." She pointed to a stack on the bedside table.

Tamara opened the book. The yellowed pages whispered their age, and the spine creaked from overuse. How many times had Clint read that very story? The pictures had faded to muted colors of mossy greens, rusty reds and powder blues, but the story still captivated Mandy.

Tamara started with "Once upon a time…"

"No." Mandy stopped her. "You gotta turn the light off."

"I won't be able to read in the dark," Tamara argued.

"The night-light will come on. Uncle Clint reads like that to me." Mandy stared up at her. "Puh-leeze…"

Clint's heart melted like an ice cube in the middle of summer. Maybe he'd made as much of an impact on Mandy as she had on him. He doffed his cowboy hat and held it pressed against his stomach. Tamara walked toward him, clicked off the light, but didn't see him where he hid, behind the partially open door.

"I can't see the pictures," Mandy said as Tamara resumed her position on the bed. The squeaky little voice made him smile. He'd heard that comment a time or two.

Tamara sighed and shifted so that her back leaned against the white-painted headboard. Mandy curled next to her, and once more Tamara began the story.

"I don't like the dark," Mandy said, interrupting again. "Uncle Clint bought me the night-light."

His chest tightened. He remembered his first night with his niece and nephew. Mandy had cried and screamed when he turned off the light. After leaving the closet light burning all night, he'd gone the next morning to find the cutest, friendliest-looking night-light available.

"Are you scared of the dark?" Tamara asked.

Mandy nodded, her eyes solemn.

"How come?"

"I dunno."

Clint had an idea. Neal and his wife had been killed on the road in the middle of the night. The kids had been staying at a neighbor's when the call came. In the scary dark of night, Mandy's whole life had shattered.

When Tamara started reading again, his niece interrupted with "My mommy used to sleep with me when I had bad dreams."

Clint swallowed a lump of regret. Maybe he should have done that for his niece. But he struggled with what was right and wrong to do as a new, single parent. Still, he took pride in the fact that at least he was home off the range in order to be there for this pint-size kid when she had bad dreams. No matter how much he missed his carefree life, he'd always know he'd done right by these kids.

"Mommies are good about doing things like that," Tamara said. "Aren't they?"

"Uh-huh. My daddy used to give me a drink of water when I had a nightmare. He'd search my room and show me there weren't no ghosts or witches hiding."

"Do you want me to check your room for you?" Tamara asked.

"Nah, Uncle Clint already did. He's the sheriff around here. He 'rests anything that looks scary. And nothin' can happen to me."

A smile tugged at his lips, and he leaned his shoulder against the door jamb. He'd invented that little game on the spur of the moment when Mandy was frightened. It had seemed to work, so he'd kept up the charade. But he hadn't intended for a pretty female boss to find out about it. Embarrassment swelled inside him, making his face hot.

"Well, he's very brave," Tamara said.

An odd sensation made his insides warm, and his hesitation toward Tamara softened like butter at room temperature.

"Uh-huh," Mandy agreed, shifting her feet beneath the covers.

"Okay, once upon a time..." Tamara paused, glanced at Mandy, and when his niece didn't interrupt she continued. "There was a mama cat who had three baby kittens. They snuggled..."

"I miss my mama."

Tamara fell silent.

The forlornness in Mandy's voice shattered Clint. He rested his head against the cool, grainy wood of the door frame.

"I know you do, sweetheart." Tamara smoothed a lock of hair behind Mandy's little ear.

Through the crack in the door opening, he watched his niece and boss. Mandy twisted the sheet in her fists. Tamara drew her lower lip through her teeth. Her eyes glimmered with tears that caught in the soft yellow glow from the night-light.

"Tell me about her." Her voice sounded calm, and as soothing as twenty-five-year-old whiskey. "Maybe that will make you feel better, Mandy."

Clint's chest tightened. Mandy had never spoken to him about her parents like this. She'd mentioned them periodically. In fact, she often blurted out the news that her parents had died to virtual strangers. It was as if she were still trying to cope, still trying to realize they wouldn't come back home. But she'd never shared her feelings about them. He regretted that he hadn't been able to help her with that. At that moment, his appreciation for Tamara doubled, tripled, manifesting itself in respect.

He was thankful she'd hired him. Glad she'd taken the time to get to know his niece and nephew better. Appreciated her interest in Mandy.

His niece lifted a tiny shoulder. "Mama was real pretty." Her voice sounded whisper-soft. "Like you." Her gaze sought Tamara's. The little girl wiggled and shifted into a sitting position. "But she had hair like mine." She curled a finger around a tendril. "See?"

Tamara nodded. "You have very pretty hair. Pretty blue eyes. I bet you're as pretty as your mother."

"Uncle Clint says I am." Her chin quivered, and her eyes filled with tears. "I wish my mama was here."

A ball of emotion wedged in Clint's throat.

With her forefinger, Tamara scooped a fat teardrop off Mandy's rounded cheek and wrapped her arm around the girl's shoulders. "I know, sweetheart, I know."

Mandy peered up at her. "Uncle Clint said your granddaddy died. Do you miss him, too?"

"Uh, y-yes." Tamara closed the book and set it on the bedside table. "And my grandmother."

"Uncle Clint said you hadn't seen them in a long time."

"That's true."

"How come?"

"Well—" Tamara shifted on the bed "—I grew up far away from here. It wasn't always easy to come back to Texas."

"But you loved your granddaddy and grandmommy?"

"I... Y-yes. I remember when I was about your age," Tamara said as she smoothed a lock of hair off Mandy's forehead. "We stayed here some with my grandparents. My granddaddy liked to read me bedtime stories."

"The little-lost-kitten story?" Mandy asked.

"No, but something similar. He liked to laugh...." She paused. "I just remembered that. He always gave me these big hugs. And he smelled of tobacco and hay." Tamara glanced away from Mandy, her voice fading. "He smoked a pipe.... I'd forgotten that, too."

Along with Mandy's, Clint's interest grew. He didn't know much about Tamara Jo Lambert. Other than that she had a Yankee accent, hated Texas and wanted to sell the ranch. Now, he wanted to know more. For some strange reason, he wanted to know why her grandfather had lived and died alone in Texas and how she'd come to live up north. He wanted to know why she disliked the ranch. Why didn't she care about the legacy her grandfather left her?

But he sensed, too, that she had forgotten a lot about her grandfather. Maybe he could help her remember. Maybe then she'd learn to love this ranch. The way her grandfather had.

Tamara settled Mandy back onto her pillow, realigning the sheet and blanket beneath the girl's chin. "You know," she said, "when I was little, I sometimes felt lost and all alone."

Surprised, Clint leaned closer.

"You did?" Mandy asked.

"Yes."

"How come?"

Tamara shook her head. "Sometimes because I was left alone. Sometimes because I was off at school. I remember how much it hurt. But you know what I did?"

Mandy waggled her head against the pillow.

"Well, I thought about my mommy and daddy every night before I went to sleep. Then, I prayed that God would take care of them. Then, at school the next day, I'd try to do what would make them proud of me."

"Were you sad inside?" Mandy asked.

"Sometimes." Her voice broke. Through the crack, he saw her draw her lower lip through her teeth. "I cried. One time, I even got mad and threw a ball through a window."

Mandy's eyes went wide.

Clint could well imagine his spunky boss hurling a ball out of frustration, fear and anger.

"It's okay to be mad," she told Mandy. "And it's okay to be sad inside, too. But as I got older, it hurt less. Like

God had put a bandage over my heart to help it get well. And it made me stronger.''

Mandy nodded, and her eyes began to droop. Tamara bent down and kissed her forehead. "Sleep well, sweetheart.''

"G'night," Mandy whispered, and her eyes fluttered closed.

Tamara eased off the bed and tiptoed across the room. Clint backed away, wondering if he should pretend he'd never heard that moving conversation. When she pulled the door toward her, he couldn't resist saying, "Don't close it all the way."

Tamara gasped and turned. Startled, she peered through the darkness at Clint. Shadowed, he looked forbidding, leaning against the wall, his body all hard angles and raw-boned strength.

"I didn't mean to startle you," he said, in the same deep but quiet voice. He set his cowboy hat back on his head.

"I didn't know you were there." She held a hand over her fluttering heart. She moved away from the bedroom door, leaving a gap that allowed a pale glow of light to seep through. "I think she'll go to sleep now."

"Thanks, Tex." His voice warmed her.

The way he called her Tex made her insides melt like sugar in the rain. She couldn't understand it, and she didn't give herself time to mull it over.

He stretched the kinks out of his shoulders, back and neck. Tamara admired the strength in his tightly coiled muscles. He looked rock-hard, slim as a fence post but sturdy as a bois d'arc tree.

"It was nothing," she said. "I mean, I didn't mind at all. She's a sweet little girl." Making her way through the darkened den, her shoes making the only sound against the hardwood floor, she felt Clint move behind her, sensed his nearness, smelled his faint masculine scent of hay and hard work. "Well, I guess I better be getting back. It's late."

She turned at the door, and Clint almost bumped into her. He stopped short, remaining only a breath away. His size overwhelmed her. She struggled between the need to back away and the desire to reach for him.

"Uh, yeah... Okay." Clint paused, his gaze intent upon her, his warm breath wafting over her like a summer breeze. "I'll walk you back."

"Oh, you don't have to do that." She stepped backward, until her shoulders met with the front door to the cottage house. "It's not far. What could be out there?"

He tilted his head, the shadows on his face shifting as the corner of his mouth lifted in a wry grin. "You never know, ma'am. The sheriff in these parts doesn't like to take chances." His accent thickened. "Gotta keep an eye out for Injuns and scalawags. Gotta protect my womenfolk."

Her breath caught, then escaped as laughter bubbled within her. "You heard?"

"Yep." His smile stretched across his face, lifting his mustache, crinkling the corners of his eyes. "I hope you didn't mind. I listened in to make sure Mandy was doing okay." He leaned one arm against the doorjamb and stared down at her. "You were real good with Mandy. I appreciate all you're doin'."

The look in his eyes and the warmth in his voice made her realize she should leave, throw open the door and race the short distance between the cottage and the main house. She should barricade her heart, but somehow she knew Clint's gentle tenderness had already stormed the fortress around her heart.

Clint watched her, knowing he should see her home, knowing he should let her go. But knowing and doing were two different things. And he wasn't sure he could do what he should.

Her sweet, warm scent surrounded him, blurred his logic, stirred his senses. He wanted her. He wanted to claim her for himself. He wanted to brace both hands against the door, lean toward her, draw the moment out until her body desired him as much as he craved her. Then he'd press his mouth to hers, pull her body tight against him. He imagined how she would soften against him, lean into him. And he'd kiss her, taste her, touch her. Slowly. Until they were senseless, weak with need, driven by desire. Until nature overwhelmed all their reservations and hesitations. He'd kiss her long and slow and deep, as if it would have to last them a lifetime.

It would, too. Because it could only be in his mind. It could never happen. Ever.

"Want a cup of coffee?" The sound of his own voice surprised himself. His offer shocked his senses back under control. He might not be able to have her, but he could spend time with her, he reasoned. Couldn't he?

"Coffee?" She blinked as if she'd awakened from a deep sleep. "At this hour?"

"I can't sleep," he said. "Lonely, I guess. I could use some adult company. It gets tiresome talking to cows all day and kids all night. Maybe you'd like something else...a soda?"

"Coffee would be fine." Her voice caressed him. "Do you have sugar?"

"Depends," he said.

She ducked her chin, as if guarding herself against his making another suggestive comment. "On what?"

He was tempted. God, he was tempted. But he said, "Well, Tex, depends on if the owner of this ranch left us any in the cupboard."

Chapter Five

Moonlight slanted through the sheer clouds, shifting across the velvety-black sky. A cool breeze stirred the branches of the live oaks that blocked the view of the highway, and the shadowy leaves rustled along the ground like fine Italian lace.

Tamara hunched her shoulders inside her denim jacket, one she'd found in her grandfather's closet, and warmed her hands on the sides of the mug. Wisps of steam brought her the friendly aroma of fresh-brewed coffee.

"Is it too cold out here for you?" Clint asked from behind her. His warm breath touched her neck and sent a shiver down her spine, tingling her nerves with awareness.

"No, this is fine. I'm a Yankee, remember?"

He smiled. "So you keep reminding me."

Something in his tone made it sound as if he weren't convinced. She stepped away, not sure she understood his comment. "This way, we won't wake the children... talking."

"I doubt Ryan's asleep. He's probably plotting how to

aggravate me some more.'' He closed the screen door and moved toward the slatted-wood swing at the far end of the porch. Silhouetted in darkness, his conservative movements made him seem even larger than he was. The swing moved in the breeze on its two rusty chains. Clint brushed the seat with his hand, clearing it of any dust or dirt or leaves.

"I hope the coffee's not too strong. I'm used to making it stout enough to keep me in the saddle for twelve hours,'' he said.

"I may not sleep for days, but it tastes wonderful.'' She sipped the strong black brew to prove the truth of her words. The sugar they'd found in the pantry took the bite out of the sharp flavor. The coffee tasted different from her usual cappuccino. It made Connecticut seem far away. Somehow, though, she didn't feel lonely, here, with Clint.

She hesitated at the top of the steps, wondering if she should gulp her coffee and disappear into the darkness before the romantic lure of the surroundings swallowed her whole. But the loneliness of her grandparents' house kept her from taking that first step.

Clint motioned for her to have a seat. "I may not be a cook, but I can make one mean pot of coffee.''

She smiled at his humor and acquiesced to his invitation, telling herself they were two adults who could share a cup of coffee and have an adult conversation. That, she reminded herself, was all this was—satisfying a lonely need in each of them.

Balancing her mug, she eased onto the swing and caught the edge of the seat behind her knees. The swing wobbled, then stilled. From the corner of her eye, she saw Clint holding the arm of the swing still, helping her without touching her. His gentlemanly gesture reached a need in her. One she hadn't realized she harbored. After all, she considered herself independent and self-reliant. But Clint made her feel protected, cared for, special, not in a condescending way, but in an old-fashioned, charming way. A need, she reasoned, that must have sprung from her isolation and loneliness here in the middle of nowhere.

Coming here after her grandfather's death had been an awakening, a reopening of old wounds. Wounds that even Mandy's questions had begun to probe. Memories had started to return, things she'd forgotten about her grandparents. Things she wasn't sure she wanted to remember.

She'd been comfortable in her tiny apartment in Connecticut, familiar with her regular customers at the bookstore she managed, and content with her independent life. But Texas had been a shock. There had been the adjustment to life in the country, and she'd had no one to talk to, share with, confide in.

This Texas ranch offered no amenities other than a stocked pantry and peaceful views of rocky hillsides and far-reaching azure skies. It had been quiet. Too quiet. With no customers she could chat with about the latest bestseller. With no close neighbors who smiled congenially and discussed whether or not it would snow by morning.

But now she had someone to talk with, and an eagerness sprang within her. She convinced herself that was all it was.

Clint sat beside her. The swing fell into a gentle rhythm. He planted his boot heels against the floor planks and pushed them back and forth, to and fro, his thighs flexing beneath his jeans.

He would normally not have been her ideal confidant, but he was here, he was friendly, and he was intriguing. A mysterious mixture of traits. Some she'd expected, others she still marveled over. She'd presumed his quiet, stoic personality, the typical cowboys, with only a few *yep*s and *nope*s sprinkled in for effect, meant there wasn't much depth beneath his cool veneer. But she'd been wrong.

There was more. Much more.

She'd observed a gentleness in him as he spoke with his

niece. She'd witnessed his struggle for patience as he handled his nephew. But above all, she'd sensed his love for his new charges.

Bullfrogs croaked a discordant melody, harmonized by a symphony of crickets. It sounded like a jungle here, isolated as the ranch was from the sounds she knew, like car horns and sirens. Her gaze steadied on the silhouette of the hills to the south of them. The bushes and rocks made the terrain seem even more treacherous at night.

"This is nice," she said, interrupting the comfortable silence that had formed between them.

"A lot quieter with the kids in bed." He grinned, his white teeth flashing in the darkness.

She sensed his need for adult companionship, too. "You've had a big adjustment over the last few months."

"Yep. Some things have been easier than others." He drank deep of his coffee and stared off into the distance.

"What's been the hardest to adjust to?" she asked, imagining the children as the spur in his side.

"Losing family. Never having the chance to see them again. Or the chance to tell them I loved them." His voice cracked.

She winced at his words. She should have known; she should have been able to guess. It seemed odd. He mourned his brother's passing. She could barely remember her grandfather. Yet they'd both inherited relatives' prize possessions. "I'm sorry."

Her apology sounded inane, but she hadn't known what to say. Wanting to know more, she waited, hoped he would continue and fill the awkward pause.

He shrugged. "Nothin' for you to feel sorry for. I guess it was a shock for all of us. We were more than just brothers." His voice sounded rough as gravel. "We were friends."

It sounded like a sweet epitaph. She sensed his pain, and

wanted to help him face his memories. "Was he older or younger?"

The look in his eyes shifted to neutral now, as if the pain had dulled and allowed him to draw the information easily from memory. "Neal was two years older. We were very close."

"And you worshiped him." She could easily see Clint, even in the shroud of darkness. He seemed tense, coiled, as if he might spring from his seat at any moment. If she got too close. She didn't figure he let people get close. He was a loner. A loner who'd had to change his ways. She wanted to reach out and smooth her hand down his arm, feel his muscles bunch in reflex. She wanted to somehow comfort him and make this transformation easier.

"Yep. I guess I did worship him. Wasn't hard to do. Neal was good at everything he put his hand to. School, football, rodeo. Girls." A wry smile touched his lips. "He taught me the ropes. Showed me how to ride, gave me advice about women." His voice flowed more easily, as if he'd begun to relax.

She smiled then. "What did he tell you about women?"

He grinned at her. "To stay away from them."

"And did you?"

"Mostly. He was the one that got married, not me. In fact, he had to get married. He got Sarah pregnant with Ryan. They were young and in love and didn't care if they had to settle down." His smile faded. "I didn't understand his decision for a while. How he could like being tied down. I'm not sure I do now, either. It's a tough transition."

Clint raked his fingers down the length of his thighs. "But I'm awfully glad he had these kids. It's like having a piece of him left behind. Neal was my hero."

"Everyone needs a hero to look up to," she said. "You're definitely Mandy's."

He shrugged. "It's been the hardest on the kids." He tilted his head toward the house. "But they're good kids. In a way, they've made it easier to deal with my brother's death.

"I can see Neal and his wife in them." A wistful smile pulled at his lips, accentuated by his thick mustache. "The way they look and talk. Even their gestures..." His voice drifted off into the darkness.

"I think you've done a great job with them. I mean, as a single man, you probably hadn't spent much time with children."

"That's an understatement." He laughed, the sound cracking through the night's quiet, stilling the hum of insect conversations. He set his empty mug on the floor beneath the swing. "You're right, though. I hadn't spent much time with anything but a bunch of ornery cows."

"Where were you ranching then?"

"When my brother...?"

She nodded.

"In Montana. Took the authorities a week to locate me after the accident. I was out on the range with spring roundup. Aren't any phones out there. Maybe that's what I liked about it. It's a good place to get away from it all. The real world couldn't intrude. But it did. And I came home."

His pain twisted her insides, wrenching the emotions from her too. "To Georgetown?"

He nodded. "I had to sell their house in order to pay for the medical expenses before Neal and his wife..." He shrugged. "I quit riding the range. Couldn't do that any-more, with two kids on my shirttail."

"I can't imagine living beyond civilization. Without a microwave, hair dryer and alarm clock, I'd be lost." She couldn't picture in her mind living farther out than this ranch. It seemed isolated enough. "Do you miss it that much?"

"Sometimes. I miss the freedom of picking up and moving on. I miss a lot about it, I guess. I try not to think about it much. I reckon it was harder on the kids.

"At first, I treated them more like livestock." He glanced at her sheepishly. "I know that probably sounds awful, but heck, that's all I knew. I herded them from place to place, fed them morning, noon and night, and kept them clean."

"Why did you want to come here?" She realized her words sounded ungrateful, and immediately she backpedaled. "I mean, I'm glad you did. But wouldn't it have been easier to have your parents' hand in raising the children?"

"My dad's been gone for years. He died of a heart attack after I had left home. My mother...well, she lived in a nursing home. Her arthritis was so bad, she couldn't live by herself. But she died not long after Neal. I guess the tragedy broke her heart. Her death was hard, but in a way she was at least out of pain. Neal's death...and his wife's..."

He drew in a deep breath and ran his fingers through his hair. "Ranching is all I know. And I needed a job. I saw your sign at Earl's."

Tamara ached for Clint. He'd lost so much. She reached out and touched his arm. The warmth of compassion swelled between them. "I'm so sorry."

"Quit apologizing. It wasn't your fault."

"I didn't know what else to say," she confessed, unfamiliar with the sense of loss and pain that Clint must feel.

"You don't have to say anything."

She placed her hand back in her lap. Where it belonged. Maybe he didn't want her sympathy.

"How have you coped with everything?" she asked.

He shrugged. A shock of brown hair fell across his forehead, and Tamara had an urge to smooth it back into place, to reassure him that she understood, to touch the wavy strands. But she kept her hands around her coffee mug.

"I focused on the kids. It kept me busy."

"I bet," she said, relieved that the somberness had eased.

He chuckled, the sound vibrating deep in his throat. "I began to see," he continued, "that they needed more than food and shelter. They needed a full-time father. Heck, I was working two jobs to keep body and soul together. But they needed more. They needed me."

He shook his head. "That took some gettin' used to." His voice dropped to a deeper, huskier tone. "But it was kind of nice to know."

Her heart opened to him then, respect filling the empty places. He was a strong man, one who probably had never imagined that he needed anyone or anything. And yet he'd given up his life for his niece and nephew, because his sense of responsibility had dictated that he had to do all he could to help them. His confession drew her toward him, like a powerful magnet, and opened the closed doors to her heart.

"I wanted us to become a real family. I thought if we lived on a ranch, together, with me a more permanent fixture around the house, then we'd bond." His brow wrinkled into a frown as he looked at her. "We've got a long way to go, but I still think it was the right decision to come here."

Moved by his honesty, touched by his desire to build a family, Tamara wanted to reach out and touch him, comfort him in the fact that he was doing all he could. And she understood why he'd fought against her selling the ranch. Tears stung her eyes. She believed he could make them a whole family. She understood his frustration at losing the life he'd once enjoyed. She'd lost her life too, temporarily, but she had the chance to get it back. Clint didn't. His change of circumstances was permanent.

But he didn't seem bitter or angry over his decision. His unselfishness amazed her. Her father had moved her and her mother across the country to pursue his dream. Had it been selfish? It had provided them with a wonderful life-style. But what sacrifices had it caused in exchange?

Clint didn't seem resigned to his new circumstances. He seemed regretful that it had happened, sorrowful about his brother's death, and protective of his niece and nephew.

He shifted uneasily, as if the swing had become suddenly rock hard. Maybe he was uncomfortable with how much he'd shared with her. The unveiling of his heart had prob-ably made him uneasy. Tamara wanted to reassure him that he could trust her. She wanted to encourage him to forge ahead on his new path.

Before she drew a coherent thought that would have warned her of the consequences, she touched his arm. Through his shirtsleeve, his body heat warmed her fingers, and fiery tendrils spread along her nerve endings until her body roared to life. Before she could pull her hand away, he covered it with his. Her pulse quickened. A warmth swelled within her, driving out the coolness of the night.

She knew she should pull her hand away, but she couldn't, any more than she could stop breathing. She'd wanted this, needed it, and now, with their fingers entwin-ing, she didn't want to stop touching him. Warning bells clanged in her head. She had to keep this in perspective.

She was his boss. He was her foreman.

But that wasn't what kept them apart.

She was leaving for Connecticut. He was staying in Texas.

Her heart still rejected that reasoning. Her mind argued that nothing could ever develop between them. No matter how many times her heart told her this was a sweet yet strong, gentle yet roughened, cowboy. He needed a woman who could love him for who he was, not someone who loved him in spite of it.

If she was to speak, she reasoned, then maybe she'd break this spell that had imprisoned them in a throbbing heat.

Clearing her throat, she said, "I think you've done a remarkable job with your niece and nephew." Her voice sounded airy, like a breath of wind blowing a thistle bloom to the four corners of the earth. She winced, knowing she'd repeated herself, but she needed to keep to a safe subject—his kids. She pulled her hand out of his grasp, and the cobwebs in her brain disintegrated. "They've adjusted well, considering everything."

She read the frown marring his brow as doubt. "There will, I'm sure, be some difficult moments ahead, but I think it's clear how much you care for them." Her gaze met and locked with Clint's, and she faltered. "Uh, Mandy just needs love and attention."

"And Ryan?" he asked, seeming to be interested in her analysis.

"He'll come around. You'll see. All teenagers are difficult. And he has a special reason to be."

"What about me?" Clint asked. "What do you think I need?"

Her insides quivered. She struggled for a safe answer. "You need your niece and nephew as much as they need you."

"You're probably right. I do need them." He smiled. "Never thought that would happen." His eyes glinted in the moonlight. "Anything else?"

She shook her head, unable to find her voice.

The seconds passed in a nervous blur. She felt him watching her as she stared at the coffee mug in her clasped hands. The ceramic shell had grown cool. It felt as if she'd absorbed all its heat, but she knew the warmth filling her came from Clint.

He shifted in his seat, turning toward her and stretching an arm along the back of the swing. Although his arm never touched her, she felt its presence, felt his warmth as if he were surrounding her, protecting her, focusing on her with a keen interest.

Nervous, she bit her lip. She should leave. She should run for the main house. She should bolt, flee. But she couldn't.

"Heck—" he chuckled "—I've probably bent your ear in a bow knot, talking so much." He reached up and tugged gently on her earlobe.

Her own laughter caught in her throat, and awareness surged through her. He rubbed her lobe between his roughened thumb and forefinger, caressing it like a piece of satin. Her body tingled, warming her to him. When their gazes met, the tension swelled between them, and he dropped his hand back to where it belonged, on the back of the swing, inches from her.

"You're probably tired of hearing about a poor cowboy and his woes," he said, his tone light but his voice strained. "I wanna hear about you. You were sure good with Mandy. Of course, she'll be your shadow from now on."

"I don't mind. She's a sweet little girl."

"It surprised me when you remembered things about your grandpa."

"I surprised myself," she admitted. "I don't remember much. But memories keep sneaking up on me." She set the coffee mug on the floor planks beside the swing and clasped her hands between her knees. "I don't like to think back to that time. What I remember most were the arguments between my grandfather and dad. When we visited, I'd run to my parents' room and throw a pillow over my head to block out the noise.

"The tension was horrific. To me, it was a relief when we moved to Connecticut. My father was busy, but happier. At least it was quiet and peaceful and calm."

"Is that why you never came to visit your grandparents?" he asked.

She eyed him, but detected only keen interest, no disdain, no surprise. As always, Clint remained calm, alert and interested. "Yes. I had no desire to come back here. I had mostly unpleasant memories. But also, I don't think my father would have let me come. It was never mentioned. I rarely thought about Texas anymore. Until…"

"Your grandfather left you this ranch in his will," Clint supplied.

She nodded.

"Is that why you inherited it, instead of your father?"

"I guess so. Dad wouldn't have wanted it, anyway."

"Your grandfather was a good man."

"I've heard." Bitterness saturated her voice. She wished she could have removed it, but for some reason she couldn't.

"And you don't want to hear any more about him, right?"

Tamara drew in a deep breath and released it. "Everybody has different memories of people. Mine don't happen to be as flattering to Joe Lambert as yours are."

"Why? Just because he and your father argued?"

"No. Because of how much they differed."

"How's that?"

"He had different notions of how to live one's life. He was satisfied with this." She gestured toward the ranch. "He wanted my father to stay here and help him."

"And your father hated this place."

"Yes. My grandfather couldn't understand that."

"And you can't understand why he'd be content to stay here on a piece of dirt. Can you?"

She'd never thought of it that way, but Clint's words were true. She couldn't understand why he'd limited himself to this ranch. Or why he'd wanted to limit his son, too. And his almighty insistence had driven a wedge through her family. Was Clint implying she was like her grandfather? Stubborn? Set in her ways? Narrow-minded? Maybe he was right. Maybe she was like Old Joe Lambert. That didn't sit well at all inside her. She balked against the insinuation.

"Everyone has a right to choose what they want in life."

"No," he said, calm and assured. "That's not true at all. A few fortunate people have that choice. Most of us do what we have to do."

A high-pitched yipping sound made her stop and glance uncertainly at Clint. Her body tensed.

"It's okay." His slow speech and gentle voice were reassuring. "Just coyotes."

The wind picked up and stirred Tamara's hair, prickling her heated skin. Clint slipped his hand to her shoulder. He was warm and comforting, gentle yet strong. Somehow his touch reassured her that she wasn't alone. Not anymore.

Time had made the separation from her grandparents seem like more of a reprieve. But something told her that she'd missed out on a lot. Yet she didn't want to face that loss. It seemed an odd word to use for something she'd never missed before. Maybe the feeling stemmed from Clint's losses. Maybe his pain had pointed out how much she'd had, but hadn't had at all.

Now, Tamara had lost her grandfather, someone she'd only now realized had loved her as she always wanted to be loved. She felt set adrift. Her only anchor seemed to be Clint. He alone seemed to understand her loneliness, her isolation.

His warm breath danced over her skin. "So," he said,

rubbing his jaw, "that's why you want to sell the ranch and go home."

She nodded in answer to his statement.

"That's your home now," he continued, almost as if he were explaining it to himself.

Home. Somehow, thinking about Connecticut didn't fill her with longing. She brushed aside the strange thought. Of course she wanted to go home. As soon as possible. Urgency bubbled inside her. Or was it confusion?

"That's why I want to sell the ranch quickly," she added.

He rubbed his jaw. "There's a cattle auction tomorrow night. It might be a good idea to go. I could take you, and you could get a vague idea about what to expect if you sell the herd."

His invitation touched her. It was the first time he'd seemed in accord with her need to sell. He actually seemed to be helping her. Maybe now he'd try to help her get out from under this burden. She should have felt elated at the prospect, but, staring into his deep brown eyes, she wasn't.

"That would be great," she said. "The sooner we sell, the better."

She read his disappointment in the frown squinching his eyebrows together. "Gotta get back your job, huh?"

"I love my job," she said. "I'd like to buy the store one day, when I've saved enough money. Selling the ranch would give me the means.

"Where I live, in Glenridge, it's a small town, very homey. Everyone knows everyone else. People know me there."

"Sounds like Georgetown," he said. "People know you here."

She shook her head. "They knew my grandfather."

"Same thing. They care about you, because they cared about your family. I've always found that comforting.

When I first started cowboying, I'd meet an old rancher who'd worked with my dad way back when. Most times, he'd give me a chance to rope and ride for his outfit, because of my dad. Pretty soon, I could get jobs on my own merit. But I've always appreciated my dad's friends looking out for me, because they'd cared about him when they'd trailed together.''

She did not understand. Clint had followed in his father's footsteps. Though she was tempted to think his life hadn't amounted to any more than her grandfather's, she couldn't shrug off the thought that Clint was making an important difference in his niece's and nephew's lives.

"I've lived a pretty simple life," he said. "But family was always important. If I needed help, my brother pitched in for me. If my family needed help, then—''

"You were there. Like with your brother's family. Your sacrifice, giving up your career for these children, is so… Well, I can't explain how it makes me feel. It's admirable. But not everyone is like that.''

He ducked his head. "I guess you're right. That's a shame, though.'' He slanted his gaze toward her. "I guess coming here has been a big shock for you. I guess you'll always think Texas is backward, down on the totem pole a ways from the loftiness of the East Coast.''

"I wouldn't say that," she told him, defending herself. Or was she defending Texas?

"Oh?'' His brow arched.

"Well—'' she caught the glint of humor in his eyes "—okay, it's been an adjustment. There are rocks and cows and…cacti.''

He nodded solemnly. "And tornadoes and rattlesnakes.''

Her gaze shot to the floor, to look for anything slithering past, then returned to him, along with a grin. "And don't forget mesquite trees.''

"And mosquitoes." He smiled.

"And coyotes."

"And cowboys."

And cowboys. Oh, God. That was the lure. Clint was the attraction. Her smile tensed, and the corner of his mustache dropped, as his mouth had thinned into a straight line. She found herself staring at his mouth and wondering...

"Maybe you haven't stayed here long enough yet." His voice was low and husky. "Maybe with time..."

Confusion closed in on her. She shook her head and stood. The swing lurched. Clint followed after her. He grabbed her elbow and turned her to face him. The moonlight cast a pale glow over his face, illuminating his dark tan, his brown eyes that flickered like firelight.

And then he took that next step.

Shifting his feet to bracket hers, he pressed her against him. She offered no resistance. Her heart pounded in her chest. He drew a line with his thumb along her jaw, and shivers shimmied down her spine.

Before tonight, she'd recognized her desire as what it was—simple physical attraction. She'd been able to resist that, remind herself of their differences. But now, all that seemed insignificant, because they'd connected on a deeper level. It had grown into something more. He'd touched a part of her, awakened in her a need that she hadn't known was there.

Lifting her chin toward him, he tilted his head, angling his mouth above hers. She tasted his warm breath, drew it in, savored it.

"Stay," he whispered as he lowered his lips to hers.

That first touch scorched Tamara, shocked her, thrilled her. She was lost in the kiss, the swirling sensations, the hope of something she couldn't put her finger on. She inched forward, her hands curling into his shirt. A purely carnal need rocked her to her core.

Her mouth opened to his, her tongue sought the taste of

him, as her body craved his warmth. She melted beneath the onslaught of his kiss. Her legs felt weak, and she leaned against him, unable to support herself. A force took hold of her and turned her emotions upside down and inside out. As unexpected as this seemed, it also felt like the most natural response.

His kiss consumed her. It was more than physical. It created a bond between her and Clint. A bond that she hadn't expected, but seemed to have existed for a long time. She had never experienced anything like this toe-curling, hand-clenching kiss. And she didn't know if anything would ever move her more.

Slowly his embrace relaxed, but the tension inside her continued to build into a frenzy. He sprinkled kisses at the corner of her mouth and drifted down toward her neck. His mustache teased her, tempted her, tickled her. He nibbled on her ear, and she shuddered with a suppressed moan.

She arched her back, looping her arms around his neck, drawing him closer, pressing her breasts against his chest, wanting, needing more of him. He erased her pain and filled the emptiness inside her with a promise, with the warmth of a home. His lips plucked at her sensitive flesh, and her insides became a fiery combustible liquid, pooling in her center. She could no longer deny how she felt for Clint. He wasn't just a cowboy. He was more. And she wanted to know more of him. But no matter what her body and soul needed, her mind screamed for her to stop this insanity.

Her body stiffened. When she pushed against his shoulders, he raised his head.

"Clint... I..."

"What's wrong?"

"I can't. I..." She stepped back, breaking contact with him. His eyes darkened with a tortured glint of disbelief, and a frown tightened his expression. "I'm your boss."

He flinched as if she'd slapped him. Her remark had been meant for her, to get herself under control, but she regretted hurting him.

"I—I have to go. I can't stay here...can't do this." She ran into the darkness. She wouldn't be tempted to stay here. This wasn't home.

But the sad reality struck her—she had no real home.

Clint watched her go, unable to move, forcing himself not to follow. His body burned for her, trembled with suppressed desire. He cursed her. He cursed himself. He cursed God.

Then he waited for a light to flick on in the main house, so that he'd know she was safe. Safe from him.

But what about him? What had he done? He'd opened up to her. He'd shared his regrets, his hurts, his fears. He wore vulnerability about as well as he would a tuxedo. Uncomfortable with his revelations, he realized that she, too, had shared her disappointments and pain. She'd touched him in a place he'd long closed off to others.

After that one kiss, he understood how his father and brother had said goodbye to the lives on the range that they loved. Each of them had met a woman who changed him. In the blink of an eye, with Tamara's velvety-soft kiss, he'd been changed, too.

He'd kissed more than a few women in his time, but he'd never been so moved, never been so willing to toss aside good sense. Not the way he'd been with Tamara.

The name brought a smile to his lips. She was everything he didn't need. But he couldn't deny he wanted her, wanted her more than he had a right to.

Tonight, he'd lost his senses in the heat of an emotional moment to a woman who could never be his. Who never wanted to be his.

And he might have just lost his job. A lot sooner than he'd anticipated.

Chapter Six

Tamara stayed awake all night, but she couldn't blame her sleeplessness on the coffee. Her body, still aflame from Clint's kisses, simmered through the night. Her mind, confused by the turn of events, replayed those moments again and again, like an old movie. Why had she let it happen? What had she been thinking?

She hadn't been thinking. That was the problem. During the time he'd lived on the ranch, she'd developed an easiness with Clint that made her feel comfortable, accepted. It had gone beyond the relationship of owner to hired help. Regret left a cold lump in the pit of her stomach. She shouldn't have allowed him to kiss her.

Kiss her?

She'd kissed him. That she couldn't deny. The blame fell on her shoulders as much as his.

She tossed and turned. She tried to block out the images, but they haunted her. The warmth of his mouth on hers, his hands touching her, his breath, hot and urgent, on her neck, were like wisps of fog closing in on her. With utter embarrassment, she remembered those moments before, when they'd connected, understood, reached out and cared for one another.

She lay in the middle of her grandparents' four-poster bed. She wondered if they had been able to reach out and care, depend on one another, love each other, through their years of marriage. Memories of her grandparents drifted through her mind like fog, with images of gentle hugs, tender kisses and meaningful looks. As if it were a picture in her mind, she remembered driving away from the ranch with her parents and looking back through the rear window at her grandparents. They'd stood together on the porch, her grandfather's arm wrapped around her grandmother's shoulders.

Tamara believed her grandparents had stood beside each other through good times and bad, supporting, encouraging, surviving. That moment when her family left them, they'd been isolated here in Texas, away from their one and only son.

Her family had relocated to Connecticut. Somehow she'd missed having the same support system that her grandparents had shared. And she suddenly felt isolated once again. Alone.

Hours later, bleary-eyed with exhaustion, Tamara peered through the faded curtains of her bedroom. Pink tendrils of light curled over the horizon, and the sky had awakened to a pale blue. Birds chattered outside her window. A cow bawled down at the barn, calling for its morning feed.

Chores didn't drive Tamara out of bed, memories of Clint did. If she busied herself, then maybe she'd forget. If only for a little while. Frustrated with her own thoughts, she flung back the tangled covers and welcomed the morning chill on her fevered skin. She refused to let silly ideas about a cowboy sidetrack her plans. She had to sell the ranch. She had to go back to Connecticut. Where she belonged. The sooner the better.

She managed to avoid Clint for most of the day. But as the time drew near for their excursion to the cattle auction, her insides twisted into nervous knots. She headed out into the cold November afternoon and grabbed a jean jacket off the peg by the door. She thought to wait for him there on the porch, but as she did, the memory of their kiss assaulted her once again.

They'd held each other in this very spot. She remembered the moonlight filtering through the canopy of leaves and forming a gentle spotlight, as if for lovers. The kiss came back to her mind in intimate detail. She ducked her head against the brisk wind and clomped down the steps in her grandmother's boots and waited beside the truck.

"Evenin'." Clint's gravelly voice made her glance up.

She froze. For a moment, she could only stare at him. His broad shoulders, slim hips and long, lean legs made her yearn for the feel of his body pressed against hers. His warm nutmeg gaze held hers, reminding her of his gentleness, his forthrightness. He'd voiced the questions she'd hidden deep in her heart, questions she'd always been afraid to find the answers to.

Unable to get a word past the breath caught in her throat, she gave a slight nod of greeting to him. His expression seemed like a locked vault. She wondered what he thought, if he remembered the kiss the way she did.

No matter how it had affected her, she had to remember that they were going in opposite directions. He was trying to embrace his new life of responsibilities, and she was trying to turn loose of the past.

"Are you ready?" he asked. His sharp, assessing gaze made her insides tremble.

"Uh, yes, I guess so." She glanced down at her jeans and boots. "I didn't know what to wear...."

His gaze followed hers, searing her with his intensity. Her skin grew warm, as if he'd caressed her. "You look fine. No one will know you're a big Texas ranch owner."

"If you mean I look poor, then that's probably as close to the truth as you can get."

He studied her for a moment, then said, "Let's get rolling."

She nodded and climbed into the driver's seat. She pumped the gas pedal, then twisted the ignition key. The truck groaned. She kept pumping and tried the ignition again. The engine finally caught, and she drew a breath of relief.

"The truck doesn't like the cold weather much."

She nodded and shifted into gear. When she reached the end of the drive, she waited for Clint to give her directions. They drove west on a lonely stretch of highway. It took almost an hour to get to the auction site, although it seemed longer, with the silence between them as quiet and ominous as snow-filled storm clouds hovering on the horizon. By the time they arrived, the sky had turned the gray of twilight.

They entered the arena and found a seat on a hard metal bleacher. The coldness seeped through Tamara's jeans, and a chill settled into her bones. The air smelled of dirt and hay and manure. She huddled inside her coat, dipping her chin and nose into the wool scarf around her neck, not so much for warmth as to escape the gritty odors.

The auction had already begun. Two cowboys brought out a cow—er, bull, as Clint explained, into a round fenced-off area. The poor creature bawled. The auctioneer gave its vital statistics, and then the bidding commenced. The auctioneer, who looked like a character from *Green Acres*, babbled, his tongue trilling over words that sounded like a foreign language. She glanced at Clint then at the people seated around her, who all seemed engrossed in the proceedings. Finally the auctioneer clapped the gavel on a bench and said, "Sold!" The two cowboys herded the bull out of the arena, and Tamara looked at Clint.

"What happened?" she whispered.

"A bull was sold."

"But how? To whom?"

He leaned close to Tamara, his shoulder pressing against hers. He nodded toward the silver-haired woman who wore a flannel shirt and jeans. "Sold to that little lady sitting on the fourth row down there."

"But she didn't move," Tamara protested.

"Yes, she did," he whispered, his breath brushing her ear and sending wild sensations coursing down her spine. "She rubs her nose as her signal to bid, if I remember correctly. Runs her ranch all by herself. Has since her husband died from a heart attack."

"They don't hold up an auction card?" she asked, remembering going to a few auctions with her parents.

"Heck, no. The auctioneer there is Buddy Simmons. He knows everybody in these parts. And if he don't, then he'll figure out your signal soon enough."

She shook her head. This was a different world. But in some odd way it wasn't. It had the small-town feel of Glenridge, where everyone knew everyone else's business. The accents were different, as were the clothes. Maybe deep down, beneath the denim and the Southern drawls, these people were simply people.

They watched for over an hour, Clint coaching her on the finer points of cattle auctions. Soon she could decipher some of what the auctioneer said. The numbers of bids amazed her. Each cow or bull sold for more than she'd ever have anticipated. Yet Clint grumbled that prices had fallen. She was beginning to think she might do better to sell the herd at auction than to sell them together with the ranch.

By the time her backside grew numb and her fingers became stiff from the cold, Clint said, "Are you ready to head on back?"

She nodded, and slowly they made their way out of the arena and to the truck. When it started with only a small grunt of protest, she began to relax. The headlights paved the way toward the highway, and they started east toward the ranch. In a short while, they would be home, and she'd be in her warm bed. Alone. And Clint would be back at the cottage house with his niece and nephew. Out of her arms' reach. And hopefully out of her mind.

But she knew better than that.

"What are Mandy and Ryan doing tonight?" she asked, suddenly concerned that she'd taken their uncle away.

"Ryan's baby-sitting. I hope the house won't be burned down when we get back."

She looked at him, then forced her gaze back to the road.

"Sorry," he chuckled. "That was meant as a joke. I'm sure everything is fine. He's a responsible boy. He's just got growing pains."

Nodding, she realized her hands clenched the steering wheel with a powerful grip. He was right. Ryan could handle everything. Couldn't he?

The engine coughed. Tamara checked the gas gauge, which hovered at the midpoint. The power steering died, and she struggled to veer the truck toward the side of the road. Slowly the truck rolled to a stop. She glanced at Clint, and he stared back at her. The brim of his hat created shadows across his face, making him look hard and mysterious.

She swallowed. "What's wrong? We're not out of gas."

He shook his head. "I don't know." Opening his side door, he said, "I'll check the engine."

Sitting in the fading warmth of the truck, she watched Clint walk around to the front and lift the hood. Through the crack at the bottom, she could see him moving about, looking at different parts. After a few minutes, he came back and climbed in the cab.

"I think it might be the battery."

"Well, now what do we do?" She felt a small rising of panic, but Clint's calm manner soothed her nerves. At least he was with her. She didn't know what she would have done out here in the middle of nowhere by herself. Alone.

Clint glanced over his shoulder toward the highway. "It's been a while since we've even seen another car. I wouldn't hold your breath on anybody stopping out here. I say we hike up the road a ways. I think the Gabbert place is only about a mile or so. We can stop in there. Charlie will come jump us off."

His gaze narrowed on her. "But if you'd rather stay here and wait, I'll hurry as fast as I can."

"No," she said, a little too quickly. She had no intention of staying out here by herself. For a moment, she felt like Mandy, afraid of the dark. But Clint was the sheriff. He'd protect her. "I'll come with you. Wouldn't hurt to stretch my legs a bit." She made up an excuse. "It'll be warmer than staying in the truck, freezing."

He nodded, and she met him on the edge of the road. They walked side by side, their footsteps loud in the quiet of the evening. Still, they kept a good foot apart, never brushing shoulders or elbows. They walked at a fast clip that made her heart race. But it also kept her warm.

Beside her, Clint stared straight ahead, his gaze somber, his face grim, his mustache pulling his mouth down into a perpetual frown. "I guess this is as good a time as any, Tamara."

"What is it?" Her heart pounded against her breastbone. She'd noticed that he'd gone back to her name, instead of Tex. She should be glad, but she wasn't.

"I'd like to apologize," he said, his voice deep and resonant. He readjusted his hat, squaring it low on his brow.

"For what?" She tried a lofty, I-don't-know-what-you're-talking-about tone.

He scowled. "The kiss."

Her cheeks flamed, whether from his words or his intense look, she wasn't sure. Grateful for the covering of darkness, she stared straight at the ground ahead of her, unwilling to glance toward him. The heat from last night surrounded her, flared within her. She remembered without any elaboration exactly what he meant. Disappointment ruffled through her like a cold breeze. One thing she hadn't wanted from him was an apology.

"Oh, that..." she said, as if it had meant nothing. She gathered her pride around her like a parka. She swallowed the ball of cotton wedged at the back of her throat. "Well, you needn't apologize. It was...an accident, a mistake. That's all. It won't happen again."

He nodded tersely. His lips thinned to a straight line beneath his mustache.

God, all she could think about was testing that seam, making him smile with a warm kiss. Her mind slammed that door shut. There was chemistry between them that she couldn't deny, but that was all. There could never be more.

"You're right there, Miz Lambert."

His formality cut through her defenses, and she realized she'd handled the whole thing wrong. He'd wanted to discuss last night. Maybe they could have retained some form of a friendship. But she'd wounded him, intimated that their shared kiss meant nothing, that he meant nothing to her. She'd belittled what they'd shared. Okay, it had been just a kiss. Or had it? She'd felt the deep pull of something more. She'd sensed a connection forming between them. And she'd severed it with careless words and a defensive attitude. In the end, she'd only hurt him and set herself up as a hard-hearted woman who gave away kisses as easily as a vending machine gave out candy.

When she lifted her chin haughtily, she tripped over a tree root and stumbled. His hand reached out and caught her. His arm braced against her waist, and his hand curled around her upper arm. The pressure felt sure and strong. He wouldn't let her fall.

Wild, hot sensations shot through her. Her gaze met his. She found him looking at her mouth. Her insides melted beneath his hot gaze. Involuntarily she licked her dry lips. It no longer mattered what she or he had said. God, she wanted him to kiss her. She wanted him to take her in his arms, hold her tight, wrap her hair around his fingers and kiss her hard and relentlessly. But she couldn't... shouldn't...let that happen. Not again.

She stepped out of his grasp. Wrapping her arms around her waist, she started walking faster. He was the foreman, she reminded herself. She was the ranch owner.

Why did that leave her feeling empty and all alone?

Four days later, Tamara sat cross-legged on the rug, old newspapers strewn around her, cardboard boxes gaping open.

Clint had found Charlie Gabbert's ranch, and the man had driven them back to their truck, jump-started the engine and followed them back to their ranch to make sure they got home safely. There had been an awkward silence between her and Clint for the rest of the journey, but then he'd chatted with Charlie as if they were old friends. She'd felt the prick of loneliness. She didn't belong here. If it hadn't been for Clint, she'd still be sitting on the side of the road.

The door to her house swung open, and a gust of wind followed Clint inside. She glanced up from wrapping up another one of her grandparents' articles.

Over the past few days, there had been a tentative uneasiness between them. They spoke to each other only when it was necessary. Now, out of the corner of her eye, she noticed his muscles moving beneath the soft flannel shirt and straining the fabric as he closed a box.

Glancing away, she busied herself, wrapping a rusted horseshoe that had been mounted above the front door. She remembered how her grandfather had told her, "Gotta keep the ends pointed toward the ceiling, or good luck will run out."

Slowly she folded old newspaper over the horseshoe and packed it in a box with her grandfather's pipes, tobacco and wire cleaners. She planned to give the dusty books, the faded clothes and the little figurines her grandmother had collected to a retirement center. Maybe some older gentleman would like to have her grandfather's pipe fixings, too.

Clint grabbed the box off the floor and folded the lid over the carefully wrapped objects.

"Hey," she said, startled out of her memories.

He stopped and stared down at her. "What's the matter?"

"Nothing, but I—"

"I was just going to load it in the truck."

"For the retirement center?" she asked, uncertain about parting with this particular box.

"Yeah. Isn't that what you wanted me to do?"

"Yes, but..."

"What?" He seemed impatient. She figured he had chores he wanted to get to and hated this menial labor he claimed was beneath a ranch foreman.

"Well, I wanted to put something else in there."

"Where? It's full."

"I know, but..." She frowned. She had no attachments to this box of trinkets and things. What would she do with them? Give them to her own parents? They'd laugh and toss them out. But still, something kept Tamara from letting Clint take them out of her own life.

"I'm going to keep this box," she mumbled.

"Why?" he asked.

She wanted to snap back that it was none of his business. But when she looked into his brown eyes, she said, "I guess I want something to remember my grandparents by."

Self-conscious about the odd feelings she was having packing up all her grandparents' belongings, she cradled a purple glazed-ceramic glob in the palm of her hand. The glaze felt smooth, but the edges of the clay were sharp and jagged. It brought back a host of memories. She knew what Clint was thinking. She didn't care about her grandparents or this ranch. She waited for a snide comment from him.

When he didn't say anything, she glanced toward him.

"What's that?" he asked.

She chuckled and looked down at the ceramic knick-knack. "It was supposed to be an ashtray."

A softness made Clint's eyes seem like golden orbs. "Mandy brought something similar home last May from day care. She said hers was a paperweight."

Tamara smiled. "I made this, when I was about her age. I gave it to my grandfather for his pipe before..." Before her father and grandfather had argued. Before they'd moved. Before she'd hugged her grandfather for the last time. She rubbed the pad of her finger over the grooves and crevices.

As if time were spinning backward, she remembered snippets of happier days. Days that had seemed as warm as the summer sun. Her grandmother had helped her wrap the ashtray that she'd made in school in red foiled paper. Then Tamara had held her breath with anticipation as her grandfather pulled open the taped edges on his birthday present. His wide grin and crinkled gray eyes had met her expectations. He'd gathered her close in what he called a bear hug, dropped a kiss on her forehead, then proudly lit his pipe.

"Gotta try it out," he'd said, setting the wobbly ashtray on his big oak desk.

Tamara had felt as if she were glowing with pride.

The memories warmed her, and she smiled down at the hopeless glob of clay. It looked lopsided and bereft of style. But her grandfather had called it a masterpiece. Tears stung her eyes. She set it in the box she'd decided to keep and reached for a stack of books. Running her fingers over the hardbacks, she breathed in the scent of dust and mildew. She pushed them toward Clint without meeting his gaze. "I thought you'd like these."

Silently he studied the books she'd found in her grandparents' collection, about the Texas Rangers and cattle ranchers and outlaws.

"Since you have fond memories of my grandfather," she said, "and since you like Texas history..." Her voice caught.

He shook his head. "You don't have to do this."

"I want you to have them."

He touched her then, cupping her chin and lifting her face toward him, until she was looking directly into his dark, unfathomable eyes. "Thank you."

She swallowed hard and watched as he hooked the books under his arm and carried another box out to the truck. She closed the box of pipes, folding the edges over and under one another. Then she began to gather books for one box, pausing now and then to read a few lines from a classic novel, marveling that her grandparents had been so well-read—almost as surprised as she'd been when she learned Clint liked to study history.

She loaded photographs in another box, smiling at the old black-and-whites, with their rickrack edges. In each picture, her grandparents smiled. Often, the camera had caught them holding hands or with their arms wrapped around each other. Tamara sensed a wealth of love between them.

Too bad that love hadn't been handed down to her father.

Brushing her hair out of her face, she searched under her grandparents' bed for anything else that needed to be packed. She found an old shoe box that someone had covered in Christmas wrapping paper. Some of the yellowed tape had pulled loose. Curious, Tamara peeled off the tight lid. Her breath rushed out of her. Inside, she found a stack of envelopes.

Sifting through the stack, she found letters in her own childish handwriting, a few from her father and even more addressed to her father, postmarked and returned to her grandparents unopened. She sank on the bed and pressed one envelope against her heart. Why were these here? Why had they never been opened? Did she dare open one now?

Reluctant to pry but too curious to put them away, she slipped a letter out of a fragile envelope and began reading.

Dear Grandma and Grandpa,
I like skule. My techr is fun. I miss you.

Love,
Tammy Jo

She could not remember penning the words. But she recognized her own awkward writing. She figured she must have been in kindergarten. The letter looked as if it had been handled many times. She wondered if her grandparents had read and reread it over the years.

The next few letters were similar, with chaotic spelling and simplistic grammar, but they were sweet and had obviously been cherished by her grandparents. Her letters seemed to have stopped about the time she and her parents moved to Connecticut. She swallowed the lump of regret in her throat. Why hadn't she written more? Why hadn't she at least called?

She knew why. Her father had forbidden it. His anger

toward his own father had never diminished in intensity. And he'd passed that anger down to her. Somehow, as she looked back on those years, the reasons didn't seem so important. A family had been torn apart, severed. The rift had never been sealed. Nor had the anger been overcome.

Tamara felt a deep sorrow swell inside her. So much had been lost and forgotten. But for what?

Curiosity prodded her to peek at the sealed letters. She remembered the heated arguments, but she couldn't recall any specific words. What could have destroyed father-and-son relations? What could have torn apart her family so completely?

Dear Jason,
Your father is terribly sorry for what happened between you. Please don't hold it against him. We both know you have your own dreams. Imagine if one of those dreams were to die, how painful that would be.

Please, call your father and talk to him. He is so distraught over this.

We both love you. We want to know how you and Michelle and Tammy are doing in your new home. Please forgive your father for his harsh words. Please keep in contact with us.

Love,
Mother

With a trembling hand, Tamara refolded the letter and slipped it back into the envelope. She opened several more, and her grandmother's pleas continued, month after month, year after year. Another one said,

Jason, it just breaks my heart to watch your father. He is in so much pain. Please, return his phone calls. Please, talk to him.

Tamara's throat tightened as she imagined her grand-mother's anguish and her grandfather's misery. Then a different style of handwriting caught her blurry gaze. She held the returned letter in her hand. It wasn't her father's or grandmother's handwriting. It must have been her grand-father's. Old Joe Lambert. She read the postmark. He had mailed it when she was in high school.

Dear Jason,
Son, it hurts me to tell you this, but your mother passed away yesterday. I tried to call you, but I guess I can't blame you for not wanting to talk with me.

Your mother was a good woman. She was loving and kind. You were her pride and joy. Her last regret was that she had not been able to see you or your daughter, little Tammy Jo, before she passed on.

I regret much that has happened over the years. I wish to hell I could take back what I said to you that day. The silence from you over the years has taught me a difficult lesson. Still, I don't want to die without you knowing I'm very proud of you, son. No matter what path you chose for your life, even if it wasn't running the ranch with me as I'd once dreamed, I've always been and will always be proud of you.

I'm not much with fancy words, but I sure found my share that horrible day so long ago. I reckon I learned that you can't make anybody live out your own dreams. Since you'd been a youngster, I'd had high hopes that you'd wanna take over the ranch from me one day. I guess you didn't love it as much as I did. But you had to find your own way. And I respect you for that.

I wish you'd come home for your mother's funeral. I wish you'd answer my calls and my letters. I wish you'd let me see Tammy Jo again.

My love to you and yours,
Dad

Tears burned Tamara's eyes. She touched the yellowed paper with her finger, noticing the splotches in the writing from what she imagined to be her grandfather's tears. She remembered how he'd hugged her the last time she'd seen him. His arms had been gentle, his chest warm as sunshine. The lingering scent of tobacco and hay had clung to his old work shirt. Her heart ached for him, for her grandmother, for herself.

Instantly she knew why her father had never responded. *He* had always been the stubborn one. If someone went against one of his ideas, he retaliated. Tamara figured he'd served his revenge to his own parents with cold disdain.

It made her angry and sick at the same time.

As a single tear slipped down her cheek, she realized that she was as guilty as her father. She'd deserted her grandparents, just as her father had. It hadn't been her fault as a child, but as an adult she'd had plenty of time. But it had been easier not to bridge that gap. Her chest felt as if a vise had squeezed it tight. She drew a shallow, shuddering breath.

She tried to lock the guilt in her heart, keep it out of sight, hide it away where she wouldn't feel the heavy weight of it. If she put the emotion away, like her grandparents' belongings, then she wouldn't have to think about it.

But that seemed almost impossible.

Clint shoved another box into the truck and cursed. What was he, a mover or a cowboy? He didn't much feel like a cowboy these days, with the piddly work he had to do to appease Miz Tamara Lambert. But maybe it was for the best. The faster he got these chores finished, then the faster she'd move back to Connecticut, where she belonged.

Wasn't that what he wanted?

He'd noticed, though, that she'd begun to hold on to the past, instead of shoving it away. Could she cling to her history? Could she learn to cherish her family's ranch? Could she fall in love with—?

That was the most ridiculous thing he'd thought of in a long while. He shook his head and headed back into the house, out of the cold. Her need to hold on to a few measly items, and her gift of a few books to him, had gone to his head...or his heart.

Wondering what boxes she wanted loaded next, he went in search of her. Hearing a rustling of paper from a back room, he followed the sound. When he tracked her down, he said, "What do you want done with these boxes?"

He stopped abruptly when he saw the look in her eyes. It took the starch right out of his irritation. It was that same little-girl vulnerability he'd learned to recognize in Mandy. "What's wrong?"

She shook her head. Light reflected a glimmer of a tear in her eye. His heart contracted. What the hell should he do now? His first instinct was to take her in his arms and comfort her. His second instinct, and a far better one, was to run. But he couldn't. He'd never been able to turn his back on a weepy female, even though they always made him uncomfortable as a Sunday suit. With Tamara, even more so.

Taking hesitant steps toward her, he edged closer and closer. She was sitting on a wide bed and staring down at a box in her lap. Something sentimental, he figured. He started to sit beside her, but thought better of it. Instead, he knelt in front of her, reached out, then withdrew his hand, thinking it unwise to touch her.

"Can I do something?" he asked, doffing his hat. He held it in his hands, shifting it from one to the other.

Again she shook her head.

He peered through the fall of her dark hair. Her nose had turned red, and a tear nestled in the corner of her mouth. He couldn't help it, and he damn sure should have reconsidered, but he touched his thumb to that tempting corner and wiped away the tear. She sniffed, and his hand cupped the side of her face.

He didn't know why, but he felt a real tenderness toward this woman. That seemed foolish or foolhardy—he wasn't sure which, or if there was even a difference. Maybe he only felt loyalty toward her because she'd hired him. Maybe he felt sorry for her because she was far from home. Maybe he felt far too much for her.

"Oh, Clint." Her voice cracked. She wrapped her hand around his wrist. "Do you know what I found?"

"What?"

"Letters." She swallowed hard. "Letters from my grandparents to my dad."

"About what?"

"No, you don't understand." She held one out to him. "Letters that my father never opened. He just returned them."

Clint shifted onto the bed and wrapped his arm around her. She tilted her head and rested it in the crook of his shoulder. "I'd always heard my father's side, why he'd been so angry at my grandfather. But I'd never thought about them...my grandparents...how they'd felt, what they'd gone through."

He rubbed her arm idly, concentrating on her pain, but not knowing what to say to help her. When she turned, he felt the soft curve of her breast brush his arm. He stared into Tamara's deep, sorrowful blue eyes, ignoring his own lust, focusing on her grief. She'd lost family. And for the first time, she'd started to grieve.

He knew all too well what that felt like.

"Thank you," she whispered. "I'm sorry I…"

"Shhhh…" He pressed his finger to her warm, supple lips. "Don't apologize. It's okay. I know how you feel. Losing those that you love is hard. You have to cry for them. For yourself."

"But how can you grieve for someone you don't know?"

She pressed herself against him, and he felt her shudder. He wrapped his arms around her, holding her close to his heart. As the moments lingered, her body remained close to his. He felt her breasts soft and lush against his chest. With his arms about her, she felt small, vulnerable. He wanted to protect her, to shield her from any more pain. It was the same feeling he felt for Mandy.

But more.

Because with Tamara, his body responded the way a man's naturally did to a woman's. His gut clenched as he fought the familiar tightening, the heat, the desire building inside him.

When she looked up at him, though, he was helpless to resist. He found himself drawn to her. His gaze focused on her parted lips. He wanted to taste her again. He wanted to feel her respond once more. He wanted her to know there was more to Texas than ranches and cacti and cows. More than pain and sorrow.

And he kissed her. More than that, she kissed him back. Their lips blended. Their breath came together. She clutched at him. Her fingers dug into his shirt, pulling him closer, showing him her need. Instinctively he knew she wanted to be close to someone, to feel the warmth she'd missed.

He'd had the same need over the past few months. But

this was more than that. He wanted more. He wanted to form a family. Could Tamara be a part of that?

He'd sacrificed his career, his life, for his family. Willingly. Family meant everything to him. For so long, he'd lived selfishly apart from his family. Now he was struggling to hold the bits and pieces of his family together through the pain and strife. But Tamara was pushing hers away. Would she push him away, too?

His heart had begun to open to Tamara. Probably because she seemed more orphaned than his niece and nephew. For some reason, he wanted her to stay. Here. On the ranch.

With him.

It made no sense. If he stopped to think about it, he would have guessed he'd gone loco. Instead, he stood and grabbed her hand. "Come on."

"Wh-what? Where are we going?" she asked, following after him.

He remained silent, his hand holding on to hers. He would show her that this ranch had been intended for her to keep, not to throw away, or to sell. That this land, this ranch, was her inheritance.

And it was his last bit of hope.

Chapter Seven

Stunned by Clint's kiss, and by his abrupt change, Tamara sat in his pickup and stared at him. "Where are you taking me?"

"You'll see." He kept his gaze trained on the road and drove fast. The silence sounded ominous.

The landscape whizzed past her window. The sun bored through the glass. She felt prickly-hot, as if her skin were melting off her body. But was that from the heat in the truck, Clint's sudden anger, or his sizzling kiss?

Why had she let him kiss her *again?*

Why had she kissed him back *again?*

She had no answers. Confused, her mind spun with all that had transpired, from her discovery of the family letters to Clint's kiss. Her chest ached with the knowledge that her father had not responded to her grandparents' pleas. Her body yearned for the comfort and security of Clint's arms once again.

She glanced over at his profile. Strong and confident, with a steel-trap jaw and a proud forehead, he appeared angry, frustrated, incensed. But why? What had she done?

She hadn't rejected him. Although she should have pushed him away. Instead, she'd pulled him closer.

Was he angry at himself? Or at her? She fought the urge to ask. She wasn't at all sure she wanted to know. But she had a feeling she would find out soon enough.

When he stepped on the brake and slowed the pickup, she glanced from side to side. The gate he turned the truck toward made her blood chill. The wrought-iron entrance had rusted where the white paint had peeled over the years. She missed reading the name as they drove under it, but she stared out the windshield at the cemetery.

The grave sites were meticulously cared for. Although the grass had faded to a dull brown with the change in the weather, bunches of wilted, windblown flowers dotted the ground at each tombstone or cross, where loved ones had remembered those they mourned. Clint drove slowly down the gravel path winding through the rows of final resting places, jouncing over the ruts. The cemetery seemed as old and forgotten as the letters she'd found, as her grandparents had been. She wondered if they had felt lonely and isolated long before they died. The thought made her heart contract.

She clenched her hands into fists, fighting the urge to cry. Her body tensed. Now she knew exactly what Clint had in mind. And she didn't like it. Her Lambert streak of stubbornness rebelled.

"Clint, take me home."

"To Connecticut?" he asked, his tone sarcastic.

She frowned at him. "You know what I mean."

"No, I don't." He pulled off to the side of the road and parked in the dry grass.

In this out-of-the-way place, weeds threatened to overtake the landscaping. The wind blew against the truck, making a forlorn cry.

Clint shifted in his seat and faced her. "And I don't know what the hell you want, either."

For only the second time, she saw anger flare in his eyes. Before, when she'd put Mandy and Ryan at risk, she'd understood his anger, accepted it, even. Now, it stunned her, made her recoil.

"The ranch is *not* your home. You've made that perfectly clear. But what *do* you want, Tamara? I think it's time you figured that out."

"I know what I want." Fury burned inside her at his audacity. "I want to sell the ranch. You just refuse to believe that."

"Yeah, I do."

"Not everybody has a family like yours, Clint," she said.

"You mean two orphaned kids and an uncle trying to hold the whole thing together? Or do you mean a family that has love?"

She glanced away from him. She didn't want to argue with him. She wanted to leave.

"If you want to sell the ranch so bad, then how come you fell into my arms? How come you cried at the truth of your family's past? How come you looked to me to soothe that pain? How come you kissed me back?"

His questions reverberated in the confines of the truck and echoed in her mind. Her heart pounded, drumming against the wall of her chest as if it would burst forth. She grabbed the door handle and pushed open the truck's passenger door. "Leave me alone, Clint Morgan."

"No, Tex, I won't."

His use of that nickname made her slam the door shut. At that moment, she hated him. Hated what he stood for. Hated this place more than she ever had. She yearned to be home in Connecticut. To be far away from Texas and these turbulent emotions.

His door clicked shut, and she heard the soft tread of his boots crunching the grass. He came around to her side of the truck, but she refused to look at him. She crossed her arms over her chest and stared out at the seemingly endless rows of graves.

"Look, Tex," he said, his voice rough with emotion, "I brought you out here because—"

"I know why you did it," she said. She glared at him then. "I don't need your help. Or anyone else's. I don't need to figure anything out. I don't need to find out what I want. I don't want the ranch. And I don't want to be here. Got that?"

He nodded. The brim of his hat shaded his eyes, but she sensed him staring down at her. Yet she could not figure out what he was thinking or how he felt. She didn't know what was going on in her own mind or heart, either. The tumultuous emotions frightened her.

"Yeah, I got it. You don't want to face the pain from your past." He leaned against the side of the truck and propped his elbow on the hood. "You don't want to face that maybe things were different than what you'd been told. You're afraid, Tex."

"Of what?" she asked with a challenging lift of her chin.

"Go find out for yourself." He nodded his head toward a narrow foot path. "Your grandparents' graves are that way."

She hesitated. The thought of peering down at the graves made her pulse race, and she didn't understand why. But to prove Clint wrong and to show herself that she could face anything, she pushed away from the truck and headed down the path. Alone.

Clint waited and cursed himself. He shouldn't have brought her here. He should have simply walked away.

As the first few minutes ticked by, he began to doubt his own wisdom. Bringing her here, to where her grandparents were buried, wouldn't accomplish anything. But in his heart he knew she cared about them. He'd seen it in her eyes, tasted it in her tears. And for some reason, he wanted to force it into the light, make her face it. For some stupid reason, he thought her love for them would make her stay.

The fall breeze had a tinge of a winter bite, but the sun's rays slanted down toward him with a keen ferocity. He readjusted his Stetson and caught sight of Tamara tramping back up the path. Her hands were clenched, and her jaw was set.

When she reached him, she propped her hands on her hips. "I can't believe this. It's horrible. Why would they let weeds take over back there?"

"There's no one to take care of it."

"Why not? Who's in charge of caring for the cemetery?" she asked, her face flushed with anger.

He scratched his jaw with his thumb. "Nobody."

"Nobody?" she repeated. "What do you mean?"

"Tex, this is a country cemetery. There aren't guards on duty or a gravedigger standing by. There's probably only a funeral out here every few months or so. Families take care of their kinfolk's graves."

"You're kidding?"

He shook his head. "That's how it's done in small towns or country cemeteries. And there aren't any Lamberts around to care for the plots."

"That's ridiculous. So they just let it look as if we don't care?"

He stared at her until her own words sunk into her conscience.

Her eyes widened. Her jaw flexed. "I know what you're thinking, Clint. And it's not true." She leaned over the bed of the truck. "I'll take care of it. Do you have a hand shovel or trowel back here?"

"For what?" he asked.

"For digging up weeds."

He rummaged around in his tool kit, sifting through pliers and wrenches, but couldn't find any gardening tools. "How about a screwdriver? You can dig with it."

"I guess it'll have to do." She took it from him and retraced her steps back down the path.

This time he followed, surprised by her anger, which showed definite promise. By the time he caught up with her, she was already kneeling beside her grandmother's tombstone. Next to it was the raw dirt of her grandfather's fresh grave. With quick, precise movements, Tamara chopped at the hard-packed earth and yanked weeds out of the soil. When she sniffed and wiped her face with her shirtsleeve, Clint bent to help her with the task of pulling weeds.

"I didn't know," she said.

He plucked a withered dandelion. "Know what?"

"Know there was no one to do this. I didn't know how much I'd missed...." She stopped and clamped her lips together.

Finally she sat back on her heels and stared at the grave. He knelt beside her and placed a hand on her arm. He sensed the struggle inside her. He wanted to help. But he didn't know how.

With Mandy, he could hold her until she stopped crying. But Tamara seemed to huddle inside herself and want to be left alone.

"What do you miss, Tex?" he asked, not knowing what to do or say, but knowing he couldn't remain silent any longer.

She shook her head. "It doesn't matter."

"Yes, it does. To me."

She sniffed again. With a dirt-smudged finger, she touched the marble stonework and traced the letters of her grandmother's name and the years of her birth and death.

"I didn't know when my grandmother died. My mom

told me years later. I was in college by then. They only found out when an attorney contacted them with the information."

"Do you remember much about her?" Clint asked.

She lifted her chin toward the sun and closed her eyes. "I remember her smile. It warmed me. She used to play with my hair, twirling my curls around her fingers and braiding it down my back." She bowed her head and rolled the stem of a faded buttercup between her fingers. "I wish I had known her better.

"I wish I had seen my grandfather again, too. If only I'd come back to see them. If only I'd been able to tell them I loved them."

"I know how you feel," Clint said. "When my brother died, I had a lot of if-onlys. If only I'd visited them more often. If only I'd spent the last Christmas with them as they'd suggested, rather than staying in Montana and rounding up frozen cows. If only... But you can't keep saying that to yourself."

"What do you say?" she asked, piercing him with a painful blue stare.

"You forgive yourself. And you move on. You remember them through memories and pictures. You say you love them in a whole different way."

Her expression closed suddenly. It was like a book being shut.

He rushed on to say, "I took my niece and nephew. Every day that I care for them, I'm telling my brother and sister-in-law that I love them."

She leaped to her feet. A darkness clouded her face. "I know what you want, Clint Morgan. You want me to stay here on the ranch. And you'll use any method to accomplish that. Well, I'm not staying."

He grabbed her arm before she could turn away. "Did you figure it out, Tamara?"

"Figure out what?"

"What you're afraid of."

She tried to pull out of his grasp, but he held her fast against him. He stared down at her. Her chest heaved with each breath. "You're afraid you're like your grandfather, Old Joe. You think he wasted his life here. But you're really much more like your own father, full of anger and resentment. Old Joe wasn't like that at all. Maybe you're afraid you're finding that out, living here. But the truth is, you're afraid to feel."

"You're wrong." She tugged on his hold again, but he wouldn't let her go.

"You're afraid you might get attached to this place. Or even to me. You're afraid of loving something or someone that might have the power to hurt you."

He released her, but before she could move away, he wrapped his arms around her. He kissed her. Fast. And stopped just as quickly. Before she could say another word, he set her away from him and walked up the path to the truck and waited for her there.

Thanksgiving prompted ideas of family. Or lack thereof, in Tamara's case. Thanksgiving represented the Pilgrims' survival in their homeland. Maybe this one would proclaim her survival over Texas. Thanksgiving stood for togetherness. But it also personified Tamara's lonely existence.

The awkward silence between her and Clint had continued over the past twenty-four hours. She would have kept to herself in the solitude of her grandparents' home, but Mandy had asked her to go to her Thanksgiving program.

Three days before the actual holiday, Tamara accompanied the Morgan family to the school cafeteria. She tried to focus on the decorations of orange, brown and red crepe paper, but she was far too aware of Clint.

They had not spoken of the cemetery since he took her

back to the ranch. And they had not mentioned the kiss, either. But she'd thought of it. And Clint's words.

Now, here among the throngs of children and proud parents, she felt isolated. Distant. Alone. People she didn't know stared at her. Folks she barely recognized greeted her. But she didn't know them. And she wasn't a part of Clint's family.

Not that she wanted to be.

She shook off her melancholy with her usual shrug of indifference. But this time she knew it mattered more than she cared to admit, because she felt the gaping hole in her soul. She began to believe that maybe Clint was right. Maybe she was afraid of caring for others.

She'd loved her grandparents and her parents. But when they lived in Texas, there had only been strife. She had seen less of her parents once they moved to the East Coast and they grew busy with their own careers. But it had been soothing to Tamara. The quiet peacefulness had comforted her.

Or had she only learned not to care anymore? To hide within herself and shut out any conflicts or discord? To be self-sufficient? The questions pounded in her head. She blocked them out, not wanting to examine herself any more.

"Looks like the whole town turned out," she commented, trying to distract her own thoughts.

"Usually does," Clint said. "These are big doing's here. Can't miss a chance for free pumpkin pie."

When the lights finally dimmed and the curtain opened, Clint, Tamara and Ryan stood at the back, straining their eyes for a glimpse of Mandy.

"Hi, Uncle Clint!" His niece waved, her voice carrying across the crowded room.

Tamara chuckled along with the audience until she saw Clint's Adam's apple bob with pride. His wide smile caught her off guard. She stood transfixed by his presence, mesmerized by his enthusiasm over his niece. She wondered if her grandfather had felt that way about her father...about her. Inside, she warmed with the knowledge that he had. She held on to that as if it were a family heirloom.

When the program ended and the last Pilgrim, Mandy, skipped offstage, Clint urged them to get in line for pie.

"Hey, Uncle Clint, can I go with my friends?" Ryan asked, suddenly not quite as sullen as before.

"Who?" Clint asked.

"Some of the guys—you know, Mark and Steve."

"Where are you going?" he asked.

"I don't know. Just around. I'll catch a ride out to the ranch with them."

Clint hesitated, obviously in a quandary.

"Come on, please. This is a drag."

"Fine," Clint said. "But be home by ten."

Ryan darted off, giving one of his friends a high five. Then they disappeared into the crowd. Tamara caught the crinkle in Clint's brow. She wanted to reassure him, tell him his nephew would be okay, but she didn't dare.

"Evenin', Miz Lambert."

Tamara turned toward the male voice. "Hello, Mr. Jerguson," she said to her neighbor. "Mrs. Jerguson." She nodded toward the plump woman. "Thanks again for those brownies."

"I was glad to do it. Wanted to make you feel welcome, you being Joe's granddaughter and all." The gray-haired lady smiled.

"How's it goin' over your way, Clint?" Mr. Jerguson rocked back on his boot heels.

"Fine. Getting things in order."

"We saw the sign." Mrs. Jerguson's gaze darted between Tamara and Clint. "Didn't know what to think of it. I mean, lands, not havin' a Lambert as a neighbor after all these years."

"You might be interested in expanding your own ranch," Tamara suggested.

"Oh, Lord have mercy!" his wife cried. "Buster Jerguson, if you buy any more land than you know what to do with, why, I'll just up and leave you."

Tamara felt Clint staring at her with the intimacy of a lover's knowing touch. She didn't risk looking his way. The back of her neck tingled, sending sparks of awareness down her spine. Disappointment followed in its wake, as she realized that the Jergusons wouldn't want her land, either.

Buster grinned at his wife. "Now, Virginia. Ain't as bad as all that. But I'll tell you, little lady—" he turned back to Tamara "—I just couldn't swing that much right now."

"I understand," she said. "I just thought it'd be better to offer it to neighbors, rather than have somebody new coming in."

"Well, hang on to your hat, sugar. Some buyer will come along. But beware of them fancy city fellers who'll strip the land and turn it into gol-darned condominiums for retired folks."

"I hadn't even thought of that," she said, but the new idea sparked hope inside her.

After the Jergusons moved on, Tamara picked at her pumpkin pie and listened to Mandy jabber. Clint complimented his niece, but his expression was solemn as a funeral director's. Several of her neighbors and her grandfather's friends made a point of saying hello to her. At first, Tamara felt awkward, not knowing them or remembering their names.

She caught Clint staring at her. Her insides hummed. Her pulse throbbed. She glanced away and fought the urge to look at him again. She wanted this night to end, ready to get back to the ranch, back to the privacy of her own house, where Clint wouldn't bother her. But she knew that was nonsense. Without even being around, he bothered her.

But not for long. Thanks to Buster Jerguson's promising idea, she had plans. Plans that just might sell the ranch lickety-split. First thing tomorrow morning, she'd place a call to Barbara Cooper's real estate agency.

"For someone who'd rather see Texas in the rearview mirror," Clint said, his voice low, but with a hint of bitterness, "you sure are being neighborly with folks."

"I wanted the Jergusons to have a chance first." She lifted her chin. "Now I have an idea who might really be interested in buying the ranch."

"Who?" The cords along his neck were stretched taut.

"I don't know the name of a company, yet. But one of those developing retirement centers in the area. They might be a possibility. One I hadn't thought of or pursued before now."

"That wouldn't be wise." He snapped a plastic fork in two.

"Why not?" She chafed at his tone. "It's my land, I can do whatever I please with it."

He dumped the rest of his pie and its paper plate in the trash. "Yes'm, you sure can. But I'd hope, seeing that your granddaddy was revered in this town, that you might consider other ranchers first."

"Why?"

"Because selling to a development company might be detrimental to the ranchers around the Bar L. The townsfolk want expansion, because it brings in more revenue. But the ranchers want everything to stay the same. Every year, they struggle to make their places pay. There's no retirement for a rancher—they can't afford it. If you do this, you might get yourself in the middle of a feud."

"Then look out, Pa Kettle. I'm selling to the highest bidder." Instantly she knew that was the wrong thing to say.

Clint stared at her. All his patience fizzled out. He narrowed his gaze and leaned toward her. She wanted to back away, but she wouldn't give. She wouldn't retreat.

"You really don't care about this place, do you?" he asked, his voice rough. "About these people, your grandparents or their friends. You don't care about anything or anyone but yourself."

Her face flushed with anger and indignation. "That's not true."

"You can't prove it by me. What's the last thing you cared about? Your grandparents?"

His jab cut right through to her heart. Blood drained from her face. "That's enough, Clint." Her voice shook. "I care about a lot of things." Her mind raced with the possibility that Clint was right. But she wouldn't...couldn't...face that. "I cared enough about Mandy to fix her a Pilgrim costume."

He snorted at that. "That was easy. You made something. But you didn't get involved. You kept your distance. Like you keep your distance from me."

He bracketed her shoulders with his hands. A tremor rippled through her. Her pulse raced.

"You know why?" he asked. "Because you're afraid to love. And you're damn afraid you could fall in love with me. A cowboy. And that scares the Yankee socks right off you."

She shook her head. Love him? He'd gone mad. She didn't love him. She couldn't love him. It made no sense. They were from two different worlds. And they were going in two different directions.

"And you're afraid to care for the ranch," he continued. "Afraid you're going to love it as much as your grandparents did. Afraid you'd want to stay right here. But that wouldn't be acceptable to your father, would it? Or to your high standards of living.

"Well, go back to Connecticut, Tex." He used the nickname sarcastically. His tone struck her like a hand across the face. "You couldn't make it here. You're not tough enough to be a Texan. You're not strong enough to love a cowboy. Because love is hard. It hurts." His eyes flared like a red-hot flame. "But hell, if you don't love, then what's living all about?"

Clint paced from one wall of the cottage to the other side. The well-worn rug that covered the scarred hardwood floor muffled the sounds of his boots. His thoughts raced, jumping from concern to concern like a rock skipping across the water.

He'd really done it this time. He should probably pack his bags and put the kids in the truck and leave, before Tamara booted him off her property.

Her property.

She shouldn't be allowed to own even a rock of this land. She didn't care about it. She didn't deserve it.

By the time the clock on the wall showed midnight, he had a more immediate worry. Mandy had long since gone to bed, and he drew comfort from knowing she was safely tucked beneath her covers. But where the hell was Ryan? It was way past his curfew.

Berating himself for letting his nephew go off with his friends, Clint jammed his hands in his pockets. He wanted to hit something, lash out, but somewhere deep inside him he managed to slip a rope around his anger and hold it in check. Racking his brain for the last names of Ryan's friends, he wished he could call their parents. He'd already scoured the phone books, trying to jog his memory, but it hadn't helped.

Clint's shoulders knotted with tension. Fear gripped his stomach. He knew what young boys did. They drove too fast. They acted reckless, thinking they were invincible, like wild stallions. God, he'd been the same way. Once he would have laughed at his parents for feeling the way he did this very minute. But suddenly he understood where his folks' worry lines had come from. He felt himself aging five years with every passing minute.

What if something happened to Ryan? What if he was hurt? What if he was killed? Icy fear twisted around Clint's heart. It would be his own fault. He alone bore the responsibility for his nephew's welfare. He alone would bear the guilt.

Raking his fingers through his hair, Clint struggled with indecision. Never before had he wavered at a fence line. On the range, he always knew how to act and react. That gave him his answer. If a cow disappeared, he wouldn't wait until she found her way home. He'd go find her.

Now he'd go find Ryan.

Tamara walked beneath the pale moonlight, her thoughts too active for her to settle down and sleep. The flashlight she held cut a swath in the darkness, the oval yellow light illuminating the path ahead. She wandered, not knowing or caring where she went. The house had begun to close in on her, and she'd needed to escape for a breath of fresh air.

Each time she closed her eyes to sleep, she'd thought of Clint. His righteous anger. His unwavering determination. His challenge that she was afraid to love him. When she opened her eyes again, she'd seen the remnants of her grandparents' lives that still remained unpacked. A framed wedding invitation. A quilt sewn with her grandmother's own hands. A wooden deer whittled by her grandfather.

She'd pulled on an old sweatshirt and jeans to go for a walk. She hated Texas. She hated this ranch. And she hated Clint Morgan.

She couldn't...wouldn't...shouldn't...love him. But did she? She wasn't ready to even think of that possibility.

She shuddered inwardly, hunching her shoulders against the icy breeze. The cold nipped at her soul like frostbite. She'd been selfish, worrying only about herself, her needs, her desires, forgetting about family who loved her. Her grandparents had cared, and her father had rebuffed them, turned away from his upbringing. Had it been so bad growing up here? Had her father hated it as much as she did now?

Or was she realizing that she saw the ranch with her own eyes, instead of her father's?

Regret and shame settled inside her like a snowbank piling up over her heart. She'd ignored her grandparents. She could never forgive herself for that.

A thin veil of clouds shrouded the moon. The night grew darker and crisper, as a cold front blew across Texas. A clapping noise startled her until she realized the wind was lifting a sheet of metal off the roof of one of the barns, then slapping it back down in place. She reached the gate that separated the yard from the barn area. With numb fingers, she lifted the chain off the wooden peg on the fence.

The gate creaked. A coyote yipped. Tamara hesitated.

Maybe she should go back inside. But she knew what would happen—she'd lie awake miserable and frustrated. She couldn't explain it, but she wanted to walk through the still barns and think of her grandparents, wonder about the lives they'd spent happily on this ranch.

She wanted to feel at home.

For the first time, she wondered if she was doing the right thing in selling the ranch. Her grandfather had given it to *her*, not her father. What had Old Joe Lambert expected her to do with the ranch? Sell it? Keep it?

She couldn't imagine he would have thought she'd know what to do with the land and cattle. She hadn't been to Texas in years. Surely he would have realized she had no interest here, no feelings for this place.

Or did she?

She turned in a circle, her gaze skimming over the dark, looming shadows of house, barns and corrals. The air smelled of hay, cattle and cedar. She drew in a deep breath, filling her lungs with the fresh, cleansing air. She knelt and braced her denim-covered knee against the rough terrain. Her flashlight focused on a jagged rock. She picked it up and held it in her hand, rolling it over against her palm, feeling the rough, grainy surface. Slowly she let it roll at an ungainly pace down her fingers, until it fell back to the earth. She stared at her hand, now smudged with dirt.

Had Texas worn off on her, become a part of her?

Her head throbbed. Questions bombarded her brain, making her wonder about her reasons to leave, creating doubts about whether she could sell.

Why would her grandfather have thought she'd want to move back here, after all these years? How could he think she'd be happy here, far away from the life she knew?

Clint came to mind. A vivid picture. His piercing gaze penetrated her weaknesses. His smile brightened her outlook, disintegrating the clouds that hovered on the horizon of her future. The memory of his arms warmed her. The blunt truth of his words spoke to her with clarity.

Could she be happy here, with a man like him?

Brushing the dirt off her hands onto the backs of her jeans, she scattered those thoughts as if they were dust in the wind. She stood and entered the barn. The overhead bulb flickered, then glowed with a bright intensity; its whiteness dissolved all the shadows. The warmth of animals and the scent of hay surrounded her, drew her further inside.

She walked the aisle, her footsteps slow, her heart heavy. She smoothed a hand down the muscled flank of Clint's horse. The thick coat tickled her palm. Her grandfather's sorrel gelding peered over his stall door, large, soulful eyes asking her when they'd take another ride. She rubbed the velvety end of his nose.

Instead of thinking about her grandparents' lives, she found her thoughts lingered on Clint. She couldn't seem to shake him from her mind. She knew her attraction had gone beyond the physical. She cared for him. Maybe too much. And that was dangerous.

An odd sound drew her attention. Cautious, she made her way to the last stall. Straining her ears, she listened. Again a thrashing sound disturbed the quiet. She looked inside the stall. The old black cow stared back at her, eyes glazed with pain and fear. She was lying on the hay-strewn floor, her sides jolting as if an alien were inside her. Her eyes rolled, and she bellowed. The lonely, desperate sound echoed against the rafters, piercing Tamara to the core. The old cow lurched to her feet, then collapsed, moaning.

Panic shot through Tamara. This cow was having her calf. And she needed help. Fast. Tamara bolted out of the barn, the flashlight glow zigzagging over the rocky terrain. She raced toward the only person she knew who could help.

Clint.

Chapter Eight

He saw her coming. Racing toward the cottage house like a bull was on her tail. Something was wrong. Bad wrong. He jogged toward her.

"Tamara," he called, knowing she probably couldn't see him in the dark.

She paused and whirled around, flashing the light in his direction. "Clint, hurry!"

The desperation in her voice sent an icy chill through his veins. He reached her and read the fear in her eyes. "What's wrong?"

"That cow...the one you brought up..." She gulped a breath. "I think she's having trouble."

Clint was off before she finished her sentence. This was typical. Bad timing. He needed to find Ryan, not nursemaid a cow. But he couldn't turn his back on an animal in trouble. He climbed over the gate, not bothering with the chain, raced across the yard and burst into the barn. Custer, his horse, shied away. Joe Lambert's gelding neighed.

"Easy." He moved past them to the last stall on the left.

The old cow struggled to rise, straining and moaning, but between her arthritis and the contractions, she couldn't move much. His thoughts jerked back to Ryan, and his own parental duty to find him. But with no idea where to go and look, he could waste half the night in aimless searching. Here, at least, he could do something, save Tamara's investment. He offered a prayer that God looked after teenage boys and geriatric cows, then entered the stall.

"Easy, old girl, easy now." He edged toward her, knowing full well the damage a frightened cow could do to a careless cowboy. His breath came in puffs of frosted air. His lungs burned. His heart pounded. Damn, he should have checked on her when he came back from the Thanksgiving program. But he'd been so angry at Tamara, so worried about Ryan. He'd shirked his responsibilities. He should have known better. With the drop in temperature, the full moon and the changes the old cow had been showing all week, the signs should have been as obvious as the difference between a heifer and a bull.

He knelt at her hindquarters and saw two calf's feet extending. But they were the wrong damn feet. The back feet.

"What's wrong?" Tamara hesitated in the doorway.

"She's havin' the calf breech. Backwards."

Tamara knelt beside him in the hay, her face the shade of milk, her eyes wide as the moon. She swallowed hard, but when she spoke her voice was strong and sure. "Okay, what do I do?"

Instantly his respect for her grew. He shrugged off his sheepskin jacket and shoved his shirtsleeves toward his elbows. "I've got to check the calf's position." He saw Tamara flinch as he began the procedure. "I'm not hurting her."

Tamara nodded and reached out to stroke the cow's side. "It's okay," she cooed. "We're going to help you."

Clint didn't like what he saw or felt. They had to act

fast. "Get those chains and that pulley hanging on that peg."

Her gaze flicked from the cow to Clint.

"Hurry!"

Before he finished his exam, Tamara had returned with the chains, and he looped them around the calf's hind feet. Bracing his heels in the soft ground, he pulled, gentle yet firm, and the calf's hocks emerged. The cow raised her head, but could not put up any resistance. Clint knew he'd be damn lucky to save both the calf and cow. And he wanted to. For Tamara.

Using the winch and chains, he dragged the calf free of its mother. Moving fast, Clint wiped the fluid away from the calf's mouth. With a piece of straw, he tickled the black nose until the calf sneezed and its rib cage heaved. Breathing a sigh of relief, he sat back on his heels. He smoothed his hand over the calf's wet hide, then moved back to wash off his hands in a water bucket.

Drawing his first deep breath in several minutes, he shook his hands and let the coolness of the night dry the water on his skin. "That's the last calf this old cow will ever have."

"Oh, God, is she going to die?" Tamara's eyes filled with tears, and she pressed a hand to her mouth.

His heart contracted at the sight of her waterlogged blue eyes, and he placed a reassuring hand on her shoulder. She trembled beneath his touch. He wanted to pull her into his arms and comfort her. Damn, he wanted to pick up where they'd left off yesterday. But he wouldn't...couldn't.

"No, Tex, that's not what I meant," he said, his voice gentle. "She's gonna make it."

"But you said..."

He nodded. "She's just too old. I don't think it would be wise to let her calve again."

Tamara sniffed and nodded her agreement. "We almost lost them both. Didn't we?"

He gave a brief, confirming nod.

"I'm glad they're going to be okay now. They are, aren't they?" She glanced at Clint, a plea in her eyes.

"Yes. They'll be fine."

She sighed, and her shoulders sagged with relief. She stared at the cow and calf. The mama cow struggled to her feet for a good sniff and first lick of her baby. Clint's gaze was riveted to Tamara's gentle expression. He'd seen many a calf born and more than a few die, and he figured he'd see a few more on down the road. But right now, he was thanking the good Lord that He'd spared this little calf and its mama. Watching Tamara made the experience new and rewarding. Seeing through her eyes, he could remember the first time he'd seen a cow give birth. Having seen so many since then, he'd forgotten the magic, the wonder. But tonight, through her eyes, he saw the miracle for what it truly was.

When Tamara smiled, he followed the direction of her gaze. The calf struggled, rising in a rock-and-roll fashion until it stood, wobbly and uncertain, but nevertheless standing.

Tamara laughed. "Isn't he adorable?"

He smiled, savoring the joy that blossomed on her face. "Yep, but it's not a boy. It's a heifer."

"Oh, well...isn't *she* adorable?" Finally, Tamara faced him, her eyes sparkling like finely cut sapphires. "Thank you."

His brow furrowed. "For what?"

"For saving them. I wouldn't have known what to do."

"That's my job. Remember?"

"I know, but...well, I was... You really know what you're doing, don't you?"

He shrugged. "Sometimes. Sometimes not."

With cattle, he'd been lucky. With Tamara, he'd been more of a fool. And with Ryan, he'd been a complete failure. Damn. He had to go after his nephew. He had to do something. What, he wasn't quite sure.

"I've got to go," he said.

Her gaze locked with his. "What's wrong?"

He shook his head, rolled down his sleeves and grabbed his sheepskin jacket. "It's Ryan. He's not home yet."

"Didn't you say for him to be home by—"

"That's why I'm worried."

She placed a hand on his arm, and an electrical current shot through him, burning a hole through to his heart. He could ask Tamara for advice. She knew how to handle the kids. Better than him, it seemed.

"What can I do?" she asked.

"Watch Mandy for me?"

"Of course." Her brow crinkled with concern. She held on to him when he would have pulled away. "What will you do?"

"I'm gonna lasso his butt back here."

"How will you find him? Do you know where he went?"

"No." He shoved his fingers through his hair. His hand trembled, and he clenched it tight. "Jeeze, I can see him on the side of the road. Broke and bleeding." The words rushed out of him, releasing his fears, his burdens, his uncertainty.

Afraid he might lose Ryan senselessly, the way he'd lost his brother, Clint felt a chill shoot down his spine.

"Right after Mandy was born, Neal got hold of me. He asked me to be his kids' guardian if anything ever happened to him or Sarah, his wife."

He laughed—a caustic sound that clawed at his guilt. "I told him, 'Sure.' But I didn't think anything would come of it. I sure as hell didn't think they'd die and I'd have to live up to my promise."

He felt as if he'd strutted right in front of Tamara in his birthday suit, bared his soul, shown her all his weaknesses. The urge to leave grew stronger, and he took a step back.

"When the attorney called me," Tamara said, her gaze distant, "about my grandfather's will..."

Clint waited.

"He told me about my grandfather, and I was numb. I didn't feel anything. Not sorrow, not grief. Nothing. It was almost like reading about some stranger in the obituaries.

"Then I found out about the ranch. I was stunned. I sure didn't want it. I didn't want to take the time off work and come down here. But I had to. I came, and..." Her voice broke. She pinched her trembling lips together. "I... well..."

He glanced at her then, his own emotions unguarded. A tear ran down her cheek, clung to the corner of her mouth, and he brushed it away with his thumb. He wanted to run his knuckles across her smooth skin and pull her against him. But he made himself withdraw. With tear-filled eyes, she looked at him, stared into his soul, touched his heart.

His throat contracted. "And you what?"

"I started to learn about my grandfather." Her tongue darted out and licked her lips. She drew a ragged breath before continuing. "You've helped me with that. You've made me face a lot of things. I realized I'd missed a lot, not knowing him. And I know...I can't feel the way you do about your brother, but...I feel this awful loss, like I never really knew this man who loved me. And it's too late to do anything to change it."

He reached out to her then, and drew her against him. Her arms went around his waist, and she nestled her cheek into the crook of his neck, leaning against him, relying on him. He breathed in the sweetness of her scent and pressed his lips to her silky hair. His hands splayed across her back, holding her close, offering comfort to her, drawing his own comfort from her. He forced back his own emotions before they broke loose. He had to push Tamara out of his arms and go after Ryan.

"It's okay, Tex. I know," he whispered against the top of her head. "Shh..." He felt the subtle shudders ripple through her, and she snuffled against his shirt.

"I'm sorry," she said, her voice muffled.

"Don't be."

She shifted in his arms, tilting her head back to gaze up at him. He flinched, knowing she would see him broken, hurting and confused. Her embrace tightened, and he gained strength from it.

"I never...mourned my brother." He squeezed his eyes shut. "I just accepted the facts, took on his responsibilities. Just like he'd asked me to. But I never..." He shook his head and tried to pull out of her arms, but she held him tight.

"It's okay," she said. "I understand."

"I wish I did."

"You have to give yourself time to grieve," she said. "Give it to yourself, like a gift, and accept the kids. You're learning about them, as they are about you."

He nodded and cupped her jaw with his hand. "And you, Tex, have to forgive yourself. You can't live each day regretting the day before. Go on."

"Back to Connecticut?" she asked.

It was the hardest answer he'd ever had to give. It made his throat burn and his heart pound. "Yes. If that's what you want."

He knew then that he could never make her stay.

A spine-searing squeal shattered the moment.

Tamara froze.

with his only son. Or maybe it had been a simple case of letting his son choose his own life.

"Hell," Clint said, "I can't do that. And Ryan probably knows it." He slammed his fist into his other palm. "If I ignore this, he'll do it again. If I make it a showdown, I might push him further away. What then? Will he get messed up even more?"

He turned to her then, his eyes dark with confusion. "What should I do?"

His heart-wrenching tone ripped through her defenses. She wanted to help this man. She realized in that moment that she'd come to care for him. Deeply. But how could she help him? What did she know about children, especially teenagers? She didn't belong here. In Texas. Or with Clint. Did she?

"I don't know," she answered honestly. "It's a delicate situation. All I know is that Ryan's hurting, really hurting. He's had a lot to adjust to in the past six months. And so have you."

He nodded, but remained silent.

"Ryan's facing his first Thanksgiving without his parents. Being a teen is hard enough without dealing with that." She took a step toward him and risked touching his arm. "I know you love your nephew, Clint. Tell him that. That's what Ryan needs."

"He needs a real parent," he said, his face grim.

She understood his feeling of inadequacy. She'd had that more than a few times over the ranch. "He needs *you*."

He snorted.

Her grip on his arm tightened. "Go easy on Ryan. He's at a difficult stage."

"Am I," Clint said, a wry grin pulling at his mouth.

"And remember, you're only angry because you were scared. Because you care." She wanted to hold Clint now, because she cared. That frightened her.

Clint stiffened.

She stared at him. Confusion made the colors in his brown eyes shift to gold and russet. "What was that?"

"I don't know." His voice held a rough edge. Turning, he headed toward the barn door. "But I'm gonna find out."

The cool night air chilled the white heat shooting through her veins. Looking toward the highway, she saw a small sports car speed down the narrow drive, lurching over the potholes, spitting gravel behind it. The headlights broke the darkness, slicing at it in a crazy fashion. The car passed the main house and kept going at a fast clip toward the cottage. Tamara held her breath. Fear gripped her.

The car swerved to a stop a couple of feet from the porch. A low, steady beat throbbed, and made the car tremble with the noise. Clint cursed again and left Tamara to follow behind. From his stiff posture and clipped pace, she sensed that his anger was boiling close to the surface.

When he reached the car, the door swung open, and music poured out. The pale yellow inside light showed three teenage boys stifling their grins. The driver ducked his head, shielding his face with his baseball cap. Slowly Ryan dragged himself out of the back seat. He tripped, planting his hands on the ground, and his friends laughed. When he stood, Clint's nephew looked like the newborn calf, wobbly and disoriented.

He'd been drinking. A lot. She shot a look toward Clint. The moon cast shadows over his profile, angling his features, darkening his face, which already appeared stern and disapproving.

Ryan stumbled toward the cottage house, his footsteps uneven, his face pale. His friend slammed the car door, and the driver threw the car in reverse. Clint pulled Tamara out of the way, setting her behind him. Together, they watched the car race down the drive, its back end swerving, its taillights glaring a bright red.

"Wait," Clint called to his nephew, his voice deadly calm.

Ryan teetered on the top step, holding on to the hand rail for support. A cockeyed grin spread across his face.

Tamara flinched. Trouble. She had an urge to duck and get out of the way. She glanced from Ryan to Clint. In the glint of the autumn moon, the boy looked too relaxed, his posture slumped, his head wobbly on his narrow shoulders. He seemed oblivious of the tension churning the air currents into a rushing torrent. Clint's nostrils flared.

Slowly, beneath the onslaught of his uncle's glare, the teen's silly grin dwindled. Ryan belched. "What?" he asked, insolence saturating his tone.

"Where have you been?" Clint asked. A thick line of frustration threaded his words.

"Out." The boy snickered at his own cleverness.

Tamara wouldn't have been surprised if Clint knocked his nephew's block off, but his restraint impressed her. Over the past weeks, she should have anticipated this clash, but she'd hoped the angry teen would turn toward his uncle, rather than against him. Didn't Ryan understand that Clint wanted to help?

Her irritation at Ryan shifted into sympathy. He had lost his parents, his home, his friends. She understood what he must be feeling all too well. She prayed that Clint would realize that, too, that he'd reach out to his nephew in love, rather than in anger. But from the hard, withering look Clint sent his nephew, she had her doubts, and a wave of apprehension swept over her.

"Get in the house." Clint's voice sounded as raw as a rope burn. "I'll be there shortly, and you better have a civil answer."

Smirking, Ryan shrugged and turned away. Clint took a step forward, as if he'd grab his nephew by the scruff of

the neck and take him down to the shed for a good hard lesson in courtesy.

Tamara put a hand on his shoulder. "Clint…"

The screen door clapped shut behind Ryan, and Cli wheeled around. A stream of curses spewed forth. He pac back and forth along the front rail of the porch. His b heels crashed against the hard-packed earth.

"What the hell am I supposed to do with him? He s out late. Disobeys me. Gets drunk. Doesn't he kno drunk killed his own folks? I should've stopped those from driving off. But I thought I might kill 'em myse

Tamara let him rant and rave, knowing he couldn't stopped the boys as they took off, and knowing that was probably well aware of the fact that a drunk driv killed his parents. But it was better for Clint to ge his chest in front of her, rather than with Ryan. K full well that his anger stemmed from fear, she wan to work out some of his rage until he could think r

"I should blister Ryan's hide with my belt," through clenched teeth. "That's what my father w done."

Her heart cried for the boy inside the house agony of a lost childhood. Too old for childr sical games and too young to handle adult re Ryan was caught in the middle. Fear and within him.

Her heart ached for the man attempting Trapped between the roles of friend and Clint had grown up himself before he wa on parental responsibilities before he w learned the hardest part of being a par dren fail and letting go. That fine line and permitting.

Maybe her grandfather had suffer

Clint stiffened.

She stared at him. Confusion made the colors in his brown eyes shift to gold and russet. "What was that?"

"I don't know." His voice held a rough edge. Turning, he headed toward the barn door. "But I'm gonna find out."

The cool night air chilled the white heat shooting through her veins. Looking toward the highway, she saw a small sports car speed down the narrow drive, lurching over the potholes, spitting gravel behind it. The headlights broke the darkness, slicing at it in a crazy fashion. The car passed the main house and kept going at a fast clip toward the cottage. Tamara held her breath. Fear gripped her.

The car swerved to a stop a couple of feet from the porch. A low, steady beat throbbed, and made the car tremble with the noise. Clint cursed again and left Tamara to follow behind. From his stiff posture and clipped pace, she sensed that his anger was boiling close to the surface.

When he reached the car, the door swung open, and music poured out. The pale yellow inside light showed three teenage boys stifling their grins. The driver ducked his head, shielding his face with his baseball cap. Slowly Ryan dragged himself out of the back seat. He tripped, planting his hands on the ground, and his friends laughed. When he stood, Clint's nephew looked like the newborn calf, wobbly and disoriented.

He'd been drinking. A lot. She shot a look toward Clint. The moon cast shadows over his profile, angling his features, darkening his face, which already appeared stern and disapproving.

Ryan stumbled toward the cottage house, his footsteps uneven, his face pale. His friend slammed the car door, and the driver threw the car in reverse. Clint pulled Tamara out of the way, setting her behind him. Together, they watched the car race down the drive, its back end swerving, its taillights glaring a bright red.

"Wait," Clint called to his nephew, his voice deadly calm.

Ryan teetered on the top step, holding on to the hand rail for support. A cockeyed grin spread across his face.

Tamara flinched. Trouble. She had an urge to duck and get out of the way. She glanced from Ryan to Clint. In the glint of the autumn moon, the boy looked too relaxed, his posture slumped, his head wobbly on his narrow shoulders. He seemed oblivious of the tension churning the air currents into a rushing torrent. Clint's nostrils flared.

Slowly, beneath the onslaught of his uncle's glare, the teen's silly grin dwindled. Ryan belched. "What?" he asked, insolence saturating his tone.

"Where have you been?" Clint asked. A thick line of frustration threaded his words.

"Out." The boy snickered at his own cleverness.

Tamara wouldn't have been surprised if Clint knocked his nephew's block off, but his restraint impressed her. Over the past weeks, she should have anticipated this clash, but she'd hoped the angry teen would turn toward his uncle, rather than against him. Didn't Ryan understand that Clint wanted to help?

Her irritation at Ryan shifted into sympathy. He had lost his parents, his home, his friends. She understood what he must be feeling all too well. She prayed that Clint would realize that, too, that he'd reach out to his nephew in love, rather than in anger. But from the hard, withering look Clint sent his nephew, she had her doubts, and a wave of apprehension swept over her.

"Get in the house." Clint's voice sounded as raw as a rope burn. "I'll be there shortly, and you better have a civil answer."

Smirking, Ryan shrugged and turned away. Clint took a step forward, as if he'd grab his nephew by the scruff of the neck and take him down to the shed for a good hard lesson in courtesy.

Tamara put a hand on his shoulder. "Clint..."

The screen door clapped shut behind Ryan, and Clint wheeled around. A stream of curses spewed forth. He paced back and forth along the front rail of the porch. His boot heels crashed against the hard-packed earth.

"What the hell am I supposed to do with him? He stays out late. Disobeys me. Gets drunk. Doesn't he know a drunk killed his own folks? I should've stopped those boys from driving off. But I thought I might kill 'em myself."

Tamara let him rant and rave, knowing he couldn't have stopped the boys as they took off, and knowing that Ryan was probably well aware of the fact that a drunk driver had killed his parents. But it was better for Clint to get it off his chest in front of her, rather than with Ryan. Knowing full well that his anger stemmed from fear, she wanted him to work out some of his rage until he could think rationally.

"I should blister Ryan's hide with my belt," Clint said through clenched teeth. "That's what my father would have done."

Her heart cried for the boy inside the house who felt the agony of a lost childhood. Too old for children's nonsensical games and too young to handle adult responsibilities, Ryan was caught in the middle. Fear and pain warred within him.

Her heart ached for the man attempting to be a father. Trapped between the roles of friend and authority figure, Clint had grown up himself before he wanted to. He'd taken on parental responsibilities before he was ready. And he'd learned the hardest part of being a parent—watching children fail and letting go. That fine line between forbidding and permitting.

Maybe her grandfather had suffered the same dilemma

with his only son. Or maybe it had been a simple case of letting his son choose his own life.

"Hell," Clint said, "I can't do that. And Ryan probably knows it." He slammed his fist into his other palm. "If I ignore this, he'll do it again. If I make it a showdown, I might push him further away. What then? Will he get messed up even more?"

He turned to her then, his eyes dark with confusion. "What should I do?"

His heart-wrenching tone ripped through her defenses. She wanted to help this man. She realized in that moment that she'd come to care for him. Deeply. But how could she help him? What did she know about children, especially teenagers? She didn't belong here. In Texas. Or with Clint. Did she?

"I don't know," she answered honestly. "It's a delicate situation. All I know is that Ryan's hurting, really hurting. He's had a lot to adjust to in the past six months. And so have you."

He nodded, but remained silent.

"Ryan's facing his first Thanksgiving without his parents. Being a teen is hard enough without dealing with that." She took a step toward him and risked touching his arm. "I know you love your nephew, Clint. Tell him that. That's what Ryan needs."

"He needs a real parent," he said, his face grim.

She understood his feeling of inadequacy. She'd had that more than a few times over the ranch. "He needs *you*."

Clint snorted.

Her grip on his arm tightened. "Go easy on Ryan. He's in a difficult stage."

"So am I," Clint said, a wry grin pulling at his mouth.

"Just remember, you're only angry because you were scared. Because you care." She wanted to hold Clint now, because she cared. That frightened her.

His lips thinned, and a hard glint entered his eyes. "I'm angry because he disobeyed me."

"Clint..."

He raised a hand, then covered hers with his own. His fingers were warm and comforting, hard and unyielding. "I know what you're saying. I'll handle it."

His eyes softened, but the lines at the corners seemed more pronounced as if he'd aged ten years in the last few minutes. "Thanks."

"I didn't do anything."

"Enough." He stepped away from her, breaking contact. Yet the bond that had formed remained intact, joining her heart with his. "You're very perceptive." A glint of humor sparked in his eyes. "For a Yankee."

She laughed at his effort to break the tension. At that moment, she realized that Clint had opened her heart.

Shoulders squared as if he were about to challenge a man to a duel, Clint stomped into the house, taking deep breaths as he went. But Ryan wasn't a man. He was a boy.

He didn't want to do this. He wanted to be an uncle, not a parent, and joke with his nephew about rodeos and girls. But fate had taken away that chance. Now he was both father and mother. Heck of a great job he'd done so far, he thought grimly.

Tamara's words seeped into his subconscious and sapped the strength from his powerful temper. She was right—he had been worried. More than worried—anxious, fearful of what might have happened. He did love that stupid kid.

By the time he reached Ryan's room, he'd gained control of his senses. Anger still simmered inside, but love burned brighter and stronger.

A retching sound made him halt in midstride. In the bathroom, Ryan was hugging the toilet like a life preserver. Clint clamped a hand on his nephew's shoulder and held him steady over the commode. It was a young man's rite of passage. One Clint had been through a few times. It was a damn good teaching tool all on its own. The rest of his anger fizzled.

"What's wrong?" Mandy asked from behind him, yawning.

"Nothing, darlin'," Clint said. "Ryan's feelin' poorly, is all. He'll be okay. I'll take care of him. Go on back to bed."

Reluctantly Mandy returned to her room, and Clint breathed a sigh of relief. Hopefully he wouldn't have to explain anymore.

When Ryan finally rested his head against the coolness of the commode, Clint handed him a glass of water, then sat on the edge of the counter and crossed his arms over his chest. "I know you're not feeling good right now, but I want you to listen up."

The boy squinted at his uncle, his eyes bloodshot, his face drawn and pale.

"You're gonna feel pukey for a few hours. And tomorrow you're gonna wish you never drank..." He leaned forward. "What was it? Beer?"

Ryan swallowed hard. "Whiskey."

"Well, if that doesn't teach you, nothing will." Clint scowled. "But that doesn't take care of you staying out past curfew. I told you to be home by ten. You didn't call or anything. So, what do you think we should do about that?"

"Shoot me." Ryan cradled his head in his hands and groaned.

"Don't tempt me." Clint stood. "You're grounded for..." What would be adequate? He'd love to lock the kid in his room until he was twenty-five, but he couldn't. He concentrated on what Tamara had said. Finally, he finished. "For a month."

Ryan's mouth dropped open, but he quickly shut it and swallowed. "Jeez..."

"I don't want to hear it," Clint said. "It's final. You do this again, and I'll make your life more miserable than you are now. And don't think I can't. Understand?"

Too weak to argue, Ryan nodded, grimacing at the pain.

"Okay, now, get yourself to bed. I've got chores for you first thing in the morning. If you're old enough to drink like a man, then you're old enough to do a man's work."

Ryan hung his head and avoided Clint's gaze.

"Call me in the night if you need anything." With that, he left his nephew alone.

He stepped out on the porch, but Tamara had already retired to her house. For a long moment, he thought about her, remembering her warm, enticing kiss. She'd revealed another side of her personality tonight. He liked her forthrightness, her honesty, her strength.

He could so easily fall in love with her. He sure never would have thought that the first time they met. But he felt himself falling every time he was around her. And he fought the urge like a wild horse struggling against a rope.

But it couldn't work. She wanted to leave. She wanted to go home to Connecticut. And he wouldn't... couldn't...ask her to stay.

Two days later, Tamara wandered aimlessly out onto the porch. The afternoon sun looked warm and inviting, but a cool breeze rustled her hair. Clint had been quiet over the past day, while he worked with Ryan on chores around the ranch. Tomorrow was Thanksgiving. It was time to go home. To Connecticut. But her heart didn't feel as jubilant as she'd anticipated.

"Hi, Tamara!" Mandy called, skipping toward her. "Wanna go look at the newborn calf?"

"Sure," Tamara said. She stepped off the porch and accepted Mandy's extended hand.

A tightness restricted Tamara's breathing. She wondered if, after she left, Mandy would remember in years to come the Pilgrim suit she'd made the little girl. Or would she be only a vague memory in the girl's childhood?

Would Clint remember her? She'd never forget him.

She knew she was falling in love with him. When she first met him, she would never have thought he'd be her type. But how could she resist falling for him? He was sweet and kind and solid. His kisses made her wild. His touch drove her crazy.

But how could he really be her type, when they wanted such different things? He wanted to establish a family. Could she want that, too? A hole in her soul cried out for it. She'd never experienced that need, never dreamed of it. Had Texas changed her? Or had it been Clint? Had he made her realize what was missing in her life—love?

"Do you think she's grown any?" Mandy asked.

Pulling her thoughts back to the here and now, Tamara said, "Well, we'll just have to see."

She opened the barn door, and Mandy scooted past her, racing down the aisle to the last stall.

"I wanna name her Daisy." Mandy peered at the baby calf, which lay curled in a lumpy black ball. The mother cow stood guard over her infant, mooing low and soft.

"She's sleepin'," Mandy whispered, loud enough to wake the dead.

"Babies sleep a lot," Tamara explained.

"She's a big baby," Mandy said.

Tamara laughed, and a whiff of smoke caught her attention. She sniffed the air, and again detected the faint odor. The hair on the back of her neck stood stiff. She glanced around, but didn't see the source. Dread shimmied down her spine. "Mandy, stay here. I'll be right back."

Pushing through the back door, she found Ryan. A puff of smoke encircled his head as he slouched against the barn wall. He held his hand behind his back and shuttered his eyes. But she knew what he was up to.

She hesitated, not knowing how to handle this or what to say. Should she confront him? Should she ignore it? Should she tell Clint?

The answer lay at Ryan's feet. Tufts of dry grass and scattered bits of hay covered the ground beneath Ryan's boots. Discarded cigarette butts dotted the small patch.

"What are you doing back here, Ryan?" she asked, approaching. "I thought you were helping your uncle."

He rolled his eyes. "What's it matter to you?"

She tried another tack. "You did a fine job helping finish the corral."

He shrugged. "Didn't have much choice."

Her nerves tightened. The anger in him made her wary. "I guess not," she said. "Your uncle did what he thought best. This is difficult for him, too."

"Yeah?" He dug the toe of his boot in the ground. "Who cares?"

"I do," she said. "And your uncle does." She ached for him, but she thought he needed to grow up a little and face facts. "Ryan, I think you need to realize you aren't the only one hurting. I know you miss your parents."

He scowled at her and crossed his arms over his chest. Gray ashes fell from his cigarette.

"But so does Mandy. You lost your parents, and that's terrible, but your uncle Clint lost someone, too, his brother. Think about that. Maybe—"

"Maybe you need to mind your own business." His tone sliced through her.

"Maybe," she said. Irritation wrapped around her spine like barbed wire. "But this ranch *is* my business, and I'd appreciate you not smoking."

"I don't care what you want."

Her patience snapped. "You'd better. If you want to ruin your lungs, then that's your problem. But this is my ranch, my barn, my land. I don't want you smoking around the horses, the cattle, the barns. It's dangerous, bad for the animals, and just plain stupid. Understand?"

He shrugged.

Her nerves frayed.

She pushed. "Understand?"

"Yeah," he said.

Anger thrummed through her. "Would you watch Mandy for me? I need to speak with your uncle."

"Gonna tattle?" the boy asked with a smirk.

"Do I need to?" she countered.

"Do whatever the hell you want. I don't care." Ryan cursed and turned away.

She shot the angry teen one last look. "Watch your little sister," she repeated. "She shouldn't be in the barn alone."

Out along the highway, Clint wrestled with a string of loose barbed wire. He'd rolled up his sleeves to his elbows. Sweat soaked his shirt, and leather gloves protected his hands. His cowboy hat sat square on his head in a no-nonsense manner.

"Clint!"

He glanced up and saw Tamara hiking toward him, her knees lifting high in the tall golden grass, her arms pumping with what appeared to be anger.

"What's up?" He dropped the barbed wire and pressed a foot against it.

"Could I have a word with you?" she asked.

His gaze narrowed, and his brow furrowed. He braced himself. He'd imagined this moment. He'd prepared himself for the news that she'd sold the ranch and was leaving.

But was he ready to leave the Bar L Ranch? Was he ready for Tamara to leave Texas?

"Sure," he managed. "What is it?"

"Well, I'm not sure if I should bring this up or not. But I was just speaking with Ryan."

What now? "And?"

"I know he's angry. I understand why, but—"

"Did he say something?" Clint's fists clenched.

"N-no. Not really." She raked her fingers through her long dark hair. "I mean, I caught him smoking."

Clint's brows shot straight up to the brim of his hat. "What?"

"He was smoking cigarettes. I caught him behind the barn." Her face flushed. "Maybe I shouldn't have said anything. Maybe I should have—"

"No, you did the right thing." He dropped his wrench to the ground. "When did this happen?"

"A few minutes ago. What are you going to do?"

Clint would sure have liked to know. How the heck was he supposed to handle this? He'd thought Ryan was improving. At least, he'd hoped so. The teen had been following the chores Clint laid out for him for the past two days. So what had happened? Whatever it was, he was about to put a stop to this behavior. Right now.

Then a bloodcurdling scream erupted down by the barn.

Chapter Nine

Stark fear sliced through Tamara. Oh, God. The barn. The children!

She and Clint took off running at the same moment. It felt like being on a treadmill—going nowhere fast. Her lungs burned. Her legs ached. Out of breath, they reached the barn together.

Flames licked at the black smoke hovering over the roof. The fiery bellow fueled by the wind turned her stomach. A cold sweat ran down her body.

Transfixed, Ryan stood a few yards away, his face tear-streaked. She felt relief that he was outside. His lanky body trembled all over, hysteria setting in. Clint grabbed the teen by his shirt. "What the hell did you do?"

"Oh, God, Uncle Clint..." He shuddered. "It happened so fast."

"Doesn't take much with old wood and straw."

Frantic, Tamara scanned the barnyard. Where was Mandy? Fear twisted her heart. Her blood turned cold as ice. She'd trusted Ryan to watch after her. She'd made a fatal error. What had she done?

"Where's Mandy?" she asked, interrupting Clint's berating his nephew.

Clint froze. When he faced her, his eyes were wild with fear. "Mandy?" Panic made his voice hoarse.

"Ryan," Tamara looked past him, "where's Mandy?" Her heart leaped into her throat. Somehow she managed, in a thready voice, to ask, "Did you get her out of the barn?"

The teen started to cry, big fat tears coursing down his cheeks. He shook his head back and forth.

Clint turned on his nephew, and Tamara raced for the barn. The entrance was clear of smoke, but once inside she saw the flames devouring the back side of the barn. Where she'd left Mandy.

She saw the little girl standing in the middle of the aisle. Heat flared, and she felt it press against her face. She could already taste the smoke. It burned her throat and stung her eyes. Icy terror pumped through her veins and froze a scream in her throat. The wooden walls crackled. Fire jumped toward the ceiling. Piles of hay and straw sizzled and popped, curling into black crisps and red-hot embers.

It was moving fast, engulfing the barn like a starving animal. Around her she heard the frightened cries of the livestock. The horses kicked at their stalls. The mother cow bellowed. The roar of flames echoed in Tamara's ears.

She raced for Mandy and grabbed her hand. "Come on! We have to get out of here."

The little girl's wide blue eyes filled with tears. Her lower lip quivered. Dragging her feet, she glanced back over her shoulder at the scrawny black calf in the stall. "What about Daisy? We gotta save her."

"I will," Tamara promised, panic making her walk faster. This was her grandfather's pride, her inheritance, burning down around her. Her one connection to her grandparents. It was hers. The animals depended on her.

She wouldn't let them die.

She pushed Mandy ahead of her. "Run! Run for the entrance!"

The little girl hesitated.

Tamara gave her an encouraging smile. "Go on. Run to Uncle Clint. I'll get Daisy."

"I tried to put it out." Ryan flinched as if Clint had struck him. "Oh, God, Uncle Clint...I did it." His face collapsed into sobs.

Clint shook his nephew, fighting the anger and frustration inside him. He wanted to throttle the boy for his irresponsibility. "Ryan, listen to me. Pay attention now."

With a glazed expression, the teen focused on Clint.

"Go to the house and call 911." He turned his nephew toward the house. "Call 911."

Ryan faltered.

Clint gave him a hard push. "Go! Now!"

He swung around and faced the barn. Smoke billowed out of the entrance. He fought down an urge to panic. Where was Tamara?

Damn! She'd gone into the barn. He knew it.

Not Tamara. Not Mandy.

He couldn't lose them. He had to get them out of there. Fast. The hay and wood were going up like firecrackers.

With that, he raced toward the barn. When he ducked inside, smoke seared his lungs. Heat pushed against him. His eyes watered. Then something bumped into his legs. He squinted down at a batch of blond curls.

Bending, he picked Mandy up in his arms. Relief flooded through him. He stepped back outside, hugging the little girl close to his chest. Moving into clearer air, he set her on the ground and ran his hands over her thin body.

"Are you okay?"

She nodded, crying at the same time.

His heart pounded. Fear stabbed at him like a seven-inch blade plunged deep into his heart. "Where's Tamara? Did she come after you?"

Mandy nodded again and pointed toward the barn. "She went to get little Daisy."

"Daisy?" Clint asked, confused.

Mandy snuffled. "The baby calf."

Clint cursed. Okay. Okay. Don't panic. His blood ran hot, boiling in his veins. He knelt beside Mandy. "I've got to go in there after her. I want you to stay here. In the open. Don't move. Understand me?"

She nodded, fresh tears brimming her eyes.

"Watch for the firemen, but stay out of the way. Don't go anywhere close to the barn. Don't go in the house, either. I don't want you in there if it catches on fire. Okay? Do you understand me, Mandy?"

"Y-yes."

"Watch for Ryan. He'll be right back. I promise I'll be back, too. With Tamara."

"And Daisy?" she asked, her broken voice melting his heart.

"With Daisy, too." With that, he ran toward the barn.

He ducked inside, the thickening smoke engulfing him. He gasped and held his breath. His lungs burned like flames. His stomach roiled. Sparks crackled as the fire burned, sizzling and popping where it devoured straw and wood like a desperate wolf on the prowl.

Squinting against the gray haze, he searched for Tamara. His gaze scoured every nook and cranny. Panicked, he thrust aside an empty oil barrel and knocked over a table of tools.

"Tamara!" he called. "Tex?" The roar of the fire swallowed his shouts. He pushed back the acrid taste of smoke and coughed.

He kicked open the first stall, praying she would be inside. Old Red squealed—a high-pitched, frightened sound. The horse backed away, his hooves slashing at the wall behind him. Clint grabbed the horse's halter and yanked on it, urging the gelding forward.

The horse reared. Clint realized that wouldn't work. He jerked off his shirt. Buttons flew like sparks. Covering the horse's face with the material, he dragged the frightened horse out of the stall. Turning the gelding toward the open doorway, away from the crackling fire, he removed the shirt and slapped the horse's rump. Old Red leaped forward. He ran for the bit of blue sky visible through the smoke screen.

Whirling back toward the blaze, Clint flung an arm across his face. The heat scorched him. Fiery red sparks fell around his shoulders. Whipping off his hat, he swiped at the ones that singed his skin with fiery needle pricks.

He stared at the back of the barn. Fear gnawed through his courage, paralyzing him for a second. Flames raged out of control. His cool confidence shattered. Where was she? He had to find her. But, God, what if he didn't?

Then he'd die trying to save her.

But what about the kids?

His mind and heart battled back and forth. Clint made the decision. Neither of them would die. He wouldn't allow it. He rushed toward the fire. Timbers and kindling fell around him. He jumped a small blazing pile of hay.

When his voice failed him and he was unable to call for her, his mind screamed out her name over and over as he searched. His eyes teared from the burning smoke, and he swiped at his face with his shirtsleeve, trying to see through the murky smoke. His heart raced. His steps quickened. He prayed. Like he hadn't prayed in years. And hoped God would listen. *Please, God, please…*

He prayed for a miracle.

He prayed for one more opportunity.

He prayed for a chance to tell Tamara that he loved her. That she belonged here. With him.

The flames growled. Sparks hissed. The hellish heat tried to drive him back.

The calf bawled, terror-stricken. Clint stumbled forward, the smoke blurring his vision. A pounding hammered to his left, and he realized Custer was trying to break free of his prison. He opened the stall, but the horse wouldn't budge, fear of fire keeping him captive.

"Go!" he yelled. Guilt tugged at him. He ought to save his own horse. It was his duty. But Tamara needed him. He drove on. He couldn't…wouldn't…take the time. Each second counted. Each second the fire burned hotter, faster, higher. Soon the barn would cave in. He had to get Tamara out first.

When he caught sight of a figure scurrying in front of the last stall, horror arced through him. What was she doing? The smoke was like a thick curtain. He bent almost double, keeping as low to the ground as possible. The heat was unbearable. Sweat slicked his skin.

He plunged his shirt inside a bucket of water. With it, he covered his nose and mouth. Then he forced himself farther into the barn. He could make out only a silhouette against the backdrop of flames. His heart jumped to his throat.

Tamara.

He raced forward. His limbs felt as heavy as the front end of the John Deere.

Above him, a beam burst open, and sparks exploded around him. He ducked and kept moving forward, ignoring the embers burning his back. He found Tamara in the stall. A hedge of fire separated them. She couldn't get out of the little room. Neither could the cow and calf.

The cow's eyes rolled. She backed away, her hindquarters scraping against the side wall. The calf cowered in the corner. Tamara was covering her nose and mouth with her arm. Coughing, she held a pitchfork in her hand. Her eyes widened when she saw Clint.

Thank God, he'd found her. Thank God, she was alive. So far. But if he didn't get her out soon, they'd be cremated alive. *Please, God, let me get her out of this inferno!*

He slapped his wet shirt at the flames. Again and again. He beat out the flames, then stepped over the threshold.

"Come on!" He held out his hand to her.

She shook her head.

"Come. Now." Each word seared his throat.

"Get the calf!" she called above the roar.

"What?" His voice came out a grating whisper.

Tears streamed down Tamara's soot-blackened face. But they were smoke tears, not terrified ones. He could tell by the determined set of her jaw. She pointed at the frightened animal. It was too afraid to move forward or backward. The little black calf trembled and bawled, and the hoarse sound tore at Clint.

Damn. He had no choice. He couldn't leave the poor thing any more than Tamara could. He'd promised Mandy. He bent over the calf and lifted it into his arms. It weighed a good hundred pounds, and Clint's muscles strained. The calf struggled. Its hooves slashed out. Clint squeezed it hard against his chest.

With a tilt of his head, he motioned for Tamara to go ahead of him. She poked the old cow in the backside with the pitchfork, not hard enough to penetrate, but enough to get her attention. Now what? All Clint needed was a charging cow. He took a step forward, but Tamara was quicker. Bravely she jabbed the old cow in the flanks again. In spite of her arthritic joints, the mother cow lurched forward. And out of the stall.

Clint nodded at Tamara. She kept after the old cow,

prodding her forward, even when the cow got scared by the flames and falling timbers.

A roar exploded in his ears, and Clint fell to his knees, managing to hang on to the calf. Pushing himself upright with his elbow, he saw the flames sink their fiery teeth into the rafters above him, gorging themselves on the roof.

Before he broke free of the suffocating smoke, he bumped into Ryan. Surprised, he stared at his nephew. What was he doing here? Anger and blame vanished. They had to get out. Now. He shoved the calf into his nephew's arms and pushed them toward the door. Tamara poked the old cow once more, dropped the pitchfork and stumbled out of the barn.

She made it. She was okay. *Thank you, God.*

A squealing whinny stopped Clint. He hesitated. He couldn't leave. Not yet. Not with his horse trapped.

Once more he faced the wall of fire crawling toward him. The horse stamped its hooves and kicked. Clint managed to grab his halter. The horse pulled back and tried to rear. Custer's eyes rolled back in his head.

Clint grabbed a saddle blanket and threw it over the horse's face. He led the gelding out into the walkway. He slapped its flanks, but the horse pranced, circling, not able to see which way it should go. Again Clint got a hold on the halter and guided the horse to the barn opening.

He coughed and choked, gagging on the smoke. He stumbled away from the barn and collapsed in the dirt. Exhaustion numbed him, blocking out the pain of minor burns. He blinked and rubbed his hand over his face. His eyes watered, trying to wash away the residue of the smoke. He had to make sure Tamara and the kids were safe. He shielded his eyes from the glare of the sun.

Squinting, he caught sight of Tamara. She lay on her side, her sides heaving with each breath, and she was coughing. He wanted to go to her, hold her, convince himself that she was fine.

He crawled toward her, his arms and legs agonizing over every inch of ground. His lungs burned. His skin felt as if it were on fire. But he riveted his attention on Tamara, needing to reach her, touch her.

A long wail sounded in his ears. He glanced over his shoulder. A red fire truck sprinted toward them. In a few seconds, it turned onto the drive, sirens screaming, lights flashing. But Clint knew it was too late to save the barn. Too late for a lot of things. This was his fault. He should have taken Ryan in hand long before. He should have been a better guardian.

"Uncle Clint!" Mandy raced toward him.

He raised up just as she plowed into him. Despite the shrieks of pain that his muscles gave, he hugged her to him, wrapping his arms around her and squeezing her tight. Touching her hair, her face, her back, he ran his hands over her and assured himself that, in spite of a little charring around the edges, she was okay.

Ryan kept his distance, still holding the little calf in his arms. He stared at the barn, his eyes red and his black-smudged face streaked with sweat and tears.

Over the shoulders of his niece and nephew, Clint looked toward Tamara. She sat, stone-faced, watching them. He tried to speak, but his voice came out like a bullfrog's croaking. He tried again and managed, "Are you okay?"

She nodded, taking away a measure of his concern. Her gaze shifted toward the barn, and guilt wrapped around his conscience like a noose. He wanted to tell her how he felt, what he wanted, what she needed. He'd promised himself he'd tell her of his love if they survived, but he felt himself backing away from that now.

What could he say to her? His nephew had set fire to

her barn. Tamara would blame Clint. How could he make it up to her? How could he erase the destruction?

Mandy wrapped her arms tighter around his neck and sobbed against his chest. He clasped her to him and rocked back and forth. "It's okay," he said. His throat burned as if flames licked at his tonsils. "It's okay."

He waved for Ryan to join them. The teen hesitated, then slowly set the calf on its feet. His face crumbled as fear and relief overwhelmed him. Collapsing beside Clint, Ryan hugged him close, whispering over and over, "I'm sorry.... I'm so sorry...."

"It's okay," Clint reassured him. "We're okay. That's what matters." He patted the teen on the back. Ryan would have to face the consequences of his actions, but right now he needed to feel safe. He needed to feel loved. And so did Clint.

Mandy buried her face against his neck. "You're fine," he said, "just fine. Uncle Clint's here to protect you. I'm here."

Forever. He'd love them, protect them, care for them, until his dying breath. And he realized, having come close to losing them, that he wouldn't have it any other way. Of course, he'd give anything to have his brother alive, but Clint wouldn't give up the sweet closeness he now shared with his kids.

This was his family. They were *his*. Even if they tried his patience and tested his nerves, he needed them, loved them with every fiber of his being. He would be lost, alone, without them.

In those few moments together, Clint realized that his father and brother had left him a legacy. Not of land and cattle and horses. But a legacy that was invaluable. Clint understood why they had left their cherished ranges for hearth and home. And now they'd passed on a generation to him, entrusted in his care, and left him to continue the cowboy traditions with his niece and nephew.

The reason his father and brother had spent hours teaching him the fine art of cowboying was that they'd loved him. They'd wanted to spend time with him, show him their love, and in doing so they'd given him a life as a cowboy. But the legacy they'd given him was love.

And he had a chance to do the same with these kids.

He wanted to pass that legacy of family love on to them. But the past few weeks had shown him he couldn't do that alone. The family circle was incomplete. And the only person who could fill the gap was Tamara. He needed her as he'd never needed any woman. He loved her with more passion and strength than the fire that blazed through the barn possessed.

With a loud rumbling crash, the rafters began to crumble, the barn caving in on itself, and his hope diminished. Guilt invaded his thoughts.

He glanced at her and saw her shoulders shake and tears course down her face. In the flicker of a flame, she believed she'd lost everything. But she hadn't. He wanted to tell her she had him and all he had to offer. If only she'd ask.

But she wouldn't.

He wished she would stay here in Texas. But he knew she wanted to go, and he would have to let her. He couldn't ask her to give up her dreams to stay here with him. As her grandfather had asked her father to do.

He knew then that all was lost. She'd return home. While he pieced together his family and his broken heart.

The barn crashed. The fireman doused the fire, keeping it from spreading to the corrals or pastures where the cattle, along with Daisy, her mama, Old Red and Clint's horse grazed. For that, Tamara had to be grateful. But her hopes, her dreams, stood in ruin. How could she sell the ranch without a barn? How could she go home?

The charred pieces of the barn were but a smoking pile of debris. With her arms crossed over her stomach, she realized that only one thing mattered. Clint and the children were safe. She watched them across the yard, crying and holding on to each other, depending on one another for support and love.

And, once again, she felt like an outsider.

Wanting, needing, but never a part.

She wanted to hug them, cry with them, hold them close to her. But she didn't dare. Each step seemed like a mile, separating her further from what she most wanted. She realized then that it wasn't Connecticut. Maybe it never had been. She hadn't been running home, she'd been running away from her inheritance, away from painful attachments.

She wanted a home, a family, loved ones who cared about her as much as she cared about them.

And she realized, as she gazed longingly at Clint and his kids, that she didn't have it here in Texas, either.

Lost and all alone, Tamara allowed the tears of loss and regret to flow.

Maybe the ranch wouldn't sell in the near future. That would give her time to think, reflect, plan. She needed time to decide what she wanted.

Chapter Ten

"**W**hat do you think we oughta do about this, Ryan?" Clint asked, the morning sun bright with newness glaring in his eyes.

Tamara watched him, her gaze flicking back and forth between uncle and nephew. There was an awkwardness between her and Clint, a hesitancy that separated them more than the width of the porch. She sensed that a barrier had been raised. This time by Clint, not her.

A cool breeze stirred the air, bringing with it a cleansing refreshment that carried the scent of burned hay and wood toward the south. They'd let the topic rest, unresolved, during the night, but with the dawning of Thanksgiving Day, the matter had to be settled. She felt too numb, too sad, to speak of it or deal with it, and too relieved that no one was injured to get beyond that precious fact.

Ryan stood, his head bowed, his shoulders slumped. "I don't know, sir."

Clint drew a deep breath. "You were damn lucky no one was hurt...or killed. If it hadn't been for..." He eyed Tamara. "...your little sister could have been..." His voice broke.

Their gazes met, locked, lingered. His eyes softened, the brown orbs deepening to the color of melted chocolate. She broke away first, her insides thrumming, her heart wrenching with pain. She swallowed the emotions surging within her.

They'd all been lucky. Apart from a few singed brows and superficial burns, everyone was fine. Even the animals had come through okay. It could have been worse. Much worse.

The thought sent a chill down her spine. If Clint hadn't come when he had yesterday, she would have been trapped. Her throat convulsed with the effort to speak. He'd saved her life. He'd risked his own life for her. Her gratefulness burned in her heart, but she couldn't find the words to express her appreciation, thankfulness...love.

Clint raked his fingers through his hair. He'd lost his hat in the fire, but that could be replaced. So could the barn, for that matter. But it wasn't a simple cut-and-dried decision when it came to what to do about Ryan. She sensed his hesitancy.

"What do you think, Tamara?" he asked, his voice coarse.

She shook her head. "I don't know."

She stared at the charred carcass of the barn. The black boards and rafters looked like rotting bones. Puddles of water speckled the ground. But Tamara could only thank God that it hadn't become their fiery grave.

In the meadow beside the highway, the mother cow chewed her cud while her calf nursed, nudging her mama's bag with her black nose. Old Red and Custer grazed along with them. None of the animals had been killed or injured.

"I know what I did was wrong," Ryan said, his voice soft and filled with remorse. "I'm sorry for it. Really, I am." He sniffed. "I could've killed somebody." He swiped at a tear with the back of his hand and drew a ragged breath. "I didn't mean for it to happen. Honest."

Tamara sensed a change in him. Maybe, after all this, he'd grown up. Maybe it was all for the best. She would gladly risk more than her barn for there to be unity in Clint's family. But would she risk her heart by taking that first step toward Clint, to bridge the gap that had opened between them?

"I'm sorry." Ryan stared at his feet. "But saying so doesn't make everything right, does it?"

"Nope," Clint said.

"I wish I could change how it is. I wish I could make you understand. I wish I could understand why I did it."

"Why were you smoking?" Clint asked. "Do you like it?"

"Nah, it kinda made me feel sick." Ryan shrugged. "I don't know, I guess I...I was mad at you, Uncle Clint."

Nodding, Clint waited. Tamara held her breath.

"You got all bent out of shape about me drinkin' and... Heck, I guess I don't blame you none. I deserved it."

"Why'd you disobey me?" he asked, his expression was stern as any father's.

The teen lifted a shoulder. "'Cause I didn't like you."

Tamara's heart stopped.

Clint's eyebrows rose. He reached up for his hat, but stopped, as if he'd realized it was no longer there. "Why? What'd I do? I didn't kill your mama and daddy. I didn't make them go away."

"I know that. But..." Ryan faltered, as if digging deep inside himself for the answer. "You didn't like me neither. Or Mandy much. I thought you wished we weren't here."

Clint's shoulders sagged. He glanced at Tamara, and she knew what he was thinking. He'd shared with her his reluctance to be the children's guardian. But she'd never imagined that the children sensed it. The anger, rebellion and fear ran deeper than the fact that Ryan's parents had been killed. Ryan resented Clint's hesitancy about being a father, just as Clint had resented it. Neither of them had been able to put a name to it, but it had driven a wedge between them.

Sorrow flowed through Tamara as she watched the two men struggle with their emotions. She prayed this would be a brand new start for them. As it would soon be for her.

Clint stepped forward and gripped Ryan's shoulder until the boy looked at him. "I'm sorry."

"You are?"

"Yep. I was wrong. I did resent y'all. At first, anyway. It wasn't against you or Mandy. It was just that I was in shock. I'd lost my brother. And all of a sudden I was a father. To kids who I knew nothing about.

"I didn't know anything about being a father. And it scared me. But not as much as when I thought I might lose one or all of you yesterday."

For a moment, his gaze wandered toward Tamara. The intensity in his eyes seared her right through to her soul. Her heart contracted. How could she go away? How could she leave Clint? But how could she stay? Would he even want her to?

His gaze shifted back to his nephew, and Clint wrapped his arm around Ryan's shoulders. "I'm glad I have y'all now. And I hope you're glad we've got each other. There's nothing I want more than for us to be a family."

Suddenly Ryan flung himself against Clint. The two men embraced, and finally Clint clapped his nephew on the back. "It's okay now. We'll work all this out. You just have to work with me, not against me. Agreed?"

Ryan nodded, and Tamara wiped away a sudden rush of tears.

"We're a family, right?" he asked.

"Yes, sir," Ryan said, his voice tight.

A family. God, Tamara wanted that, wanted to be a part of their family.

"Good. Then we'll stick together through this." Clint jammed his hands in the back pockets of his jeans and eyed his nephew.

Again Tamara felt alone, separated from what she most wanted—to belong. An intense pain sliced through her heart.

"Miz Lambert," Ryan said, looking as awkward and gangly as a pelican. "Miz—"

"I thought you were calling me Tamara, like everybody else," she managed.

He nodded. "Yes'm, but I thought after yesterday—"

"Nothing has changed, Ryan."

"I'm sorry, Miz...Tamara." He shifted from foot to foot, but his gaze met hers solidly. "I truly am. I can't say it enough. I wanna make it up to you. I'll do anything you say." His eyes filled with tears. "I did a bad thing. And I'm real sorry. I hope you'll forgive me."

She watched him, knowing the words came from his heart, not from fear of what she'd say or do but from genuine distress over what he'd done. "It was an accident, Ryan. The important thing is that everyone is all right. No one was seriously hurt. The barn can be replaced. People can't. But, yes, I forgive you."

He expelled a breath in a whoosh. "Thanks." He looked as if a burden had been suddenly lifted from his shoulders.

"We still have to figure out a punishment," Clint said, his voice hard.

"I agree," Tamara said.

"I'd like to wring your neck," Clint added, "but I can't."

Sweat popped out on Ryan's upper lip.

"We could string him up by his thumbnails," Tamara suggested, hoping to make this conversation lighter.

Ryan's eyes bulged.

Clint chuckled. "Not a bad idea."

Tamara smiled.

The teen's gaze shifted back and forth between the two adults until it registered that they were kidding. Then his eyes sparked with an idea. "I want to rebuild the barn."

She smiled wistfully. "I think you're going to need quite a bit of help for that."

"I can do it." His jaw jutted out. "Uncle Clint will tell me what to do. Won't you, Uncle Clint?"

Clint nodded at his nephew. "You're gonna have to pay for it. You'll have to work hard to pay everything back."

"I'll get a part-time job, whatever. I'll work hard. I promise. I'll make it up to you, Tamara. You'll see."

"I believe you," she said. But would she be here to see it?

The blare of a car horn sounded, and Clint glanced toward the highway. The honking continued, growing in volume as another truck, then another and another, joined in. Several cars and trucks joined the procession that paraded down her drive. A small tornado of a dust storm swirled behind the churning tires.

The cars and trucks lined up in rows. Doors swung open, and hordes of people emerged. Doors slammed, and the crowd moved toward them like the evening tide swelling toward the East Coast.

"Who are all these people?" Tamara asked.

"Your neighbors." Clint's voice sounded flat.

He'd lost all hope. It wasn't that he'd be out of work, it wasn't that his kids wouldn't have a permanent home, that made his gut double up. They'd survived so much. They'd continue to survive. But would he? He needed Tamara. And he didn't know if he could endure the pain.

Earl Watson grinned and waved at them.

Clint nodded. "Buster Jerguson and his wife are here, too." He motioned toward the couple, who carried covered dishes.

"What are they coming here for?" she asked.

"To help you out." His gaze met Tamara's. Surprise turned her blue eyes the color of bluebonnets in the spring. "That's what neighbors do around here."

"Good mornin'," Earl said, crowing loud as a rooster.

The whole group of more than twenty people gathered in front of the porch. Tamara stood stiff with uncertainty.

"Tammy Jo Lambert," Earl said, hitching up his overalls, "we heard what happened out here. And we're sure sorry you lost your barn. And all that hay. Some of us started jawin' about it being Thanksgiving. And Lord, we sure are thankful nobody was hurt. But we figured it was a time to lend a helping hand to a friend and neighbor."

"Friend?" she whispered. "But—"

"We all chipped in, and the ladies brought some grub."

Buster Jerguson clapped Earl's back. "Get to the point."

The owner of the feed store laughed. "Okay, okay. What I'm tryin' to say is we're gonna help you rebuild your barn."

"You are?" Tamara blinked as if she'd fallen into a trance. She glanced at Clint.

"Yes'm, we sure is." Earl grinned.

She looked around at all the smiling, friendly faces. "You'd give up your holiday, your hard-earned money, your time, to help a perfect stranger. Why?"

"Heckfire, Tammy Jo," Earl said, "you're our neighbor. Ain't no other reason needed than that."

Her gaze went straight to the For Sale sign along the

highway. She blinked back tears and shook her head. "I can't accept this."

"Don't you understand?" Clint asked. "They're extending their hand of friendship to you. And you'd slap it away? Just like that?"

"I didn't mean it that way. I meant..." A tear slipped down her cheek. "I can't believe this."

"Believe it," Clint said, his heart swelling with pride at the generosity of those he'd known his entire life. "Tex, you are one hardheaded woman."

She bristled at his words. "I am not."

He chuckled. Lifting his voice to the crowd gathered, Clint said, "Go ahead, folks. Let's get started."

Buster Jerguson clapped his hands together. "Whooee! We're wastin' daylight." He swiped his arm over his eyes and sniffed, loud as a hog. "Let's get to work."

The men headed toward the barn site, shovels, picks and hammers in their hands, while the women disappeared with armloads of food into her house. Clint stared at Tamara. There was so much he wanted to say to her. But how? And would it matter in the long run? She needed something far different from what he had to offer.

One lone car came up the dusty dirt drive. As it neared, Clint recognized it as Barbara Cooper's truck. His gut tightened. When the real estate agent emerged, her smile told him all he needed to know.

A contract had been offered.

Tamara would be leaving soon.

He felt the pain in his bones, as if a winter storm were approaching. This was what she wanted. This was what she'd hoped for. And he should be glad for her. But all he could feel was the pain in his own heart.

"Good morning!" Barbara Cooper practically sang as she jogged up the steps.

Clint crossed his arms over his chest and nodded.

"Have I got good news for you!" the real estate agent said.

"Did you see the barn?" Tamara asked. "Everything in it was lost."

"Oh, don't worry about it. A development company has offered a contract. The fire probably saved them tearing-down costs. They won't keep anything here, anyway."

"Not even the houses?" Tamara asked.

"Heavens, no."

"You're still going to sell?" Ryan asked, his eyes round with a mixture of surprise and hurt. "But I thought... What about us? Where are we going to go?"

"Ryan..." Clint warned his nephew.

"Ryan, listen..." Tamara started to explain. "Clint..."

He shook his head, not wanting to hear any more. His heart heavy, he turned away. He looped an arm around his nephew's shoulders and drew him down the steps and toward the barn.

"Might as well tell everybody to stop clearing the debris. The development company will just bring in heavy equipment for that," Barbara Cooper said.

Clint ignored her. If Tamara wanted to disappoint her neighbors, then she could tell them. Right now, he wanted to hit something. And he figured lifting a few heavy beams would help deplete his anger.

"Where are we going to go?" Ryan asked.

"I don't know," Clint said. "We'll work something out."

He shoved his hands into his leather work gloves. His boot heels sunk into the waterlogged ground. He lifted a charred beam and carried it to a pickup for hauling away. As he worked, grinding his teeth in frustration and straining his muscles, he watched the real estate agent talk with Tamara on the porch.

When he saw them shake hands, anger seethed inside

him. At that moment, something snapped. He couldn't let Tamara leave, not without trying to keep her here with him. Not without her knowing how he felt about her.

It was his last chance.

Tamara watched Barbara Cooper leave. For the first time in a long while, her heart felt light. Her spirits soared. She gazed out at her grandfather's ranch, at the horses grazing in the pasture, at the cow and its calf nursing. Tears stung her eyes. This time, they weren't tears of grief or sorrow or longing. They were tears of joy.

She felt free.

When she saw Clint stalking toward her, her heart stopped. His dark complexion was reddened with anger. His body looked stiff. His hands were tightened into fists. He came up the porch steps, taking them two at a time.

"Clint, I..." Her voice trailed off as he came straight for her.

His brows slanted into a deep frown. He grabbed her shoulders and squeezed. "You, Tamara Lambert, are not selling this ranch. I can't let you do it."

She raised her chin and glared right back at him. Outraged anger churned inside her. "You can't stop me. All you care about is yourself, losing this job, having this ranch turned into condominiums."

"No, I care about losing you."

"What?" Her heart turned over.

"You heard me." His scowl deepened. "I can't lose you. If you're not here, this ranch won't matter. I can't let *you* leave. You are not moving back to Connecticut. You are staying here. Where you belong. Do you understand?"

His words sounded sweet, and she knew she'd remember them forever. She nodded. "Yes."

"I won't listen to any arguments or..." His eyes widened then squinted at her. "Back up there. What did you say?"

She allowed a gentle smile. "I agreed with you, Clint Morgan."

"You did?" His grip on her shoulders relaxed. He took a step backward and released her. "How come?"

She laughed at his expression and realized her agreement must have shocked him. "Because I turned down the offer Barbara Cooper had from the development company."

"But I saw you shake hands."

"We parted as friends. I told her I'd decided not to sell the ranch."

"You're not?" he asked.

She shook her head, and a bubble of laughter rose from her throat. "I'm not selling the ranch."

He ran his fingers through his hair. "What? I mean, I'm glad—"

"You are?" she asked.

"Yes." He met her gaze solidly, the conviction in his stare made her insides ripple. "But, are you sure?"

"I'm sure."

"Are you going to sell to another buyer?"

"Nope. I'm staying here. I don't want to leave."

He stuck his thumbs through his belt loops and stared down at the ground. She wondered if he'd heard her correctly. Finally he glanced back at her. "What about your job up there?"

"What about it? You were right, Clint. I was afraid." She took a step toward him, her insides quaking with desire. "I'm not anymore."

"What are you going to do, then?"

"Run the ranch." She shrugged, uncertainty over his response overwhelming her. "There's already a fine bookstore in town, but maybe they'd like a coffee shop next door. That's the newest rage, you know."

"No. I didn't know." Clint stared at her. "Are you sure about this?" His voice drew her closer to him.

"Absolutely." She had no doubts.

"What changed your mind?"

She took a deep breath. "A lot of things. I learned this is my heritage, given to me by my grandfather." The words felt true and strong as they poured from her heart. "And it means more than I ever thought it would. You were right."

"I was?"

"Yes, you were."

"About?"

"In telling me that I was afraid. I was afraid to love something. I'd held myself apart. Loving had always hurt. But *not* loving, I realized, hurt worse."

"How did you figure that out?"

She swallowed the lump in her throat. This time, she didn't fight the tears. She let them fall. "When I thought I'd lose Mandy..." Her voice cracked. "But most of all...you."

He stared at her, his gaze softening.

It was her move now. And she did. She stepped toward him, raised up on her tiptoes and settled her body against his. She'd never been so sure of anything in her life. Suddenly she felt as if she belonged. "One other thing made me decide not to sell."

"What?" he asked, his voice hoarse. His hands touched her waist. The warmth turned her blood hot.

"I fell in love with a cowboy," she said.

His eyes turned to liquid fire. He pulled her flush against him and buried his face against her neck. His breath burned hot along her skin. "I don't want you to leave," he whispered. "I can't help it. I know it's selfish. But I... I need you. More than anything."

"I need you, too." She held him against her, wrapping

her arms about his neck, breathing in his warm, familiar masculine scent.

Then he lifted his head and stared deeply into her eyes, touching her very soul. "Tamara Lambert," he said, his voice thick, "I love you."

She swallowed a fresh bout of tears. "I love you."

"God, that sounds good. Say it again."

"I love you." She laughed. It came easier the second time, and she grinned through her tears.

He kissed her, hard and fast. When he released her mouth, she could only stare in amazement at him. He loved her. And that love consumed her.

Hammering began down at the barn, and she glanced over his shoulder at the men, who'd rolled up their sleeves to begin work. "Did you do all this?" She gestured toward her neighbors. "Get them to come here?"

"Nope. But if I'd known it would've had this effect, I'd have burned the barn long ago."

She smiled. "Just to keep your job?"

He shook his head. "To keep you." His voice sounded gravelly. "I want you."

A warmth spread through her like a wild fire.

He shifted his position, bracketing her feet with his boots. "That is, if you want me."

"Is that why you saved my life yesterday?"

"I didn't think about it like that. It was something I had to do. I couldn't have lived if you'd…" His voice trailed off. His arms tightened around her. "I've lost so much, and I couldn't bear losing you, too."

She touched her hand to his face. "I never thanked you for that. If you hadn't come—"

"Shh…" He tapped his finger to her lips. His hands closed over her upper arms. "It's over now. You're safe. I'm safe. We're all okay. But one thing isn't settled."

"What's that?"

"Can you be happy here? In Texas?"

"With you I can." She rested her hands against his chest.

"I want you to be a part of my family." His words brought the wellspring of joy inside her bubbling to the surface. He brushed the tears off her cheeks. His touch felt as gentle as a leaf falling from a tree. "Will you marry me, Tammy Jo Lambert?"

Her heart thrilled at the words. "Tammy Jo?" she asked, her ears roaring with the beat of her heart. "I never thought I'd like the sound of that."

"You like that better than Yankee?"

She laughed. "Definitely."

"So?" he asked, his brow drawing into a frown. "What do you say? Will you?"

She smiled up at him. "Call me Tex."

His grip on her tightened. "Tex." He ground it out between his teeth. His eyes glowed like amber. "Will you marry me?"

"Maybe."

He crushed her to him and kissed her. She felt the impact clean down to her toes. Her heart began to melt beneath the intensity of his embrace. His kiss was hard, unrelenting, yet exquisitely tender. Her senses whirled.

When she could no longer breathe, he broke the kiss. "Maybe?"

She swallowed hard and wrapped her arms around his neck. "Yes. That is, if we can live here, in Georgetown, on *our* ranch. With our family."

"You got a deal, darlin'."

He kissed her, sweeping away all doubts. He enfolded her in his arms, surrounding her with all the love and acceptance she'd craved for so long. He cradled her head against his chest, and she heard the steady beat of his heart.

He brushed a kiss against the top of her head. "I never understood why my dad and brother would have given up life on the range. Until I met you. And I realized I'd been the one missing out on life. Not them.''

Tightening her embrace, she gazed up at him and gave him a smile. Finally, she had a place to call home and a family all her own. She had a man who loved her, children she would help raise as her own, and neighbors who'd welcomed her. She belonged. Thanksgiving, she realized, was more than dinner, football and stuffed bellies. Thanksgiving was home and family. And Texas was where she belonged.

She'd finally found her own cowboy legacy.

Epilogue

The spicy aroma of chili filled the kitchen as Tamara stirred the meat-and-bean mixture. She glanced out the window and watched Clint walking toward the house from the barn. With his head tilted down, she couldn't see his face for the shadows his hat created. But her heart warmed at the width of his broad shoulders and his long, determined stride.

Setting the lid on the pot of chili, she met him at the door with a smile and a kiss. His arms closed about her, pulling her full against his chest. He smelled of hay and sunshine. A warmth that matched the unseasonably hot weather filled her with a familiar longing.

"Now, that's the way a cowboy likes to be greeted after a long day," he said, his mouth curving beneath his mustache.

She stepped back, and he entered the house. "How was your day?"

"Good. Got those heifers out of the far pasture." He lifted the corner of her red-checked apron. "What's this?"

"It was my grandmother's," she answered, smiling at the pleasure it brought her. "I found it on the top shelf of the pantry." She made a slow turn, rolling her hips like a hula dancer. "How do you like it?"

"It's you, darlin'." He laughed. "Where are the kids?"

She took hold of his hand, enjoying the mixture of hard, sinewy muscles and warm, tanned skin. "Mandy's in her room, playing quietly, and Ryan's doing his homework."

He raised a quizzical brow. "Any problems with Ryan?"

"Not a bit. He seems changed." She rubbed her palm across his knuckles. "You know?"

"Yeah." He smiled at her, his gaze warming. "I like it." He touched her cheek, then whisked off his hat and hung it on a peg beside the door.

She walked up behind him and wrapped her arms around him, pressing her face against his back, luxuriating in the strength of his hard muscles flexing beneath her cheek. "Dinner should be ready in a few minutes. Are you hungry?"

Turning to face her and enfolding her in his arms, he whispered against the top of her head. "Only for you, Mrs. Morgan."

She smiled up at him. "You know, we could leave the chili simmering and..."

He caught her wink and grinned. "That's my kind of woman."

Hand in hand, they walked toward their bedroom, tiptoeing past Ryan's, then Mandy's, bedroom. The carpet cushioned their footsteps.

"What about the kids, though? Will they wonder where we've gone?" Tamara asked, her body tingling with excitement.

"Don't worry. I'll lock the door and turn on the television. They won't suspect a thing."

She hugged her husband close, and her heart filled with

love. They'd been married only a month, and their honeymoon seemed to continue. Smiling to herself, she kicked off her shoes as Clint did as he'd promised. The evening newscast filled the television screen, the noise drowning a giggle that spilled out of her.

She felt like a wanton high school senior, sneaking around behind her parents' backs. Except they were sneaking around behind their kids' backs. Flushed with the heat of seduction, she started to unbutton her blouse.

"Hey," Clint said, joining her on the bed. "That's my job." He stretched his long frame out beside hers and slid his hand slowly down the length of her body, his fingers grazing the sensitive underside of her breast and her ticklish rib cage. Her nerves electrified. While he nibbled on her neck, his fingers kneaded her hip, pulling an involuntary groan from deep in her throat.

His hand stilled, and he glanced over his shoulder at the television. The fog in her brain cleared enough for her to hear the newscaster say, "A blizzard has halted everything on the East Coast."

"Do you miss Connecticut?" he asked, his breath tickling the shell of her ear.

She shook her head. "Especially not the occasional blizzards during the winter." She hugged him close, drawing in the scent of him. "I've never been happier."

"Me neither." He pressed a kiss to her cheek. "I thought my brother was nuts when he got married. But now I understand. Marriage has a lot of benefits that sleeping out with a bunch of cows doesn't have."

"Watch out—" she grinned "—you're getting dangerously close to comparing your wife to a cow."

"Never." His look of mock horror faded. The sunlight filtering through the blinds caught the glimmer in his brown eyes, making them dance like firelight. He drew a line along her jaw and down the column of her throat, his gaze following. He toyed with the bra clasp between her breasts.

"You're beautiful, Tamara." He planted tiny, tender kisses along the warm trail his finger had left. "I've never been happier. And it's all because of you, Tex."

She sifted his hair with her fingers. "Me neither, cowboy. Texas is where I always want to be. Right here with you."

* * * * *

® Silhouette®

AVAILABLE THIS MONTH FROM SILHOUETTE ROMANCE®

As seen on TV!
Free Gift Offer

With a Free Gift proof-of-purchase from any Silhouette® book,
you can receive a beautiful cubic zirconia pendant.

This gorgeous marquise-shaped stone is a genuine cubic
zirconia—accented by an 18" gold tone necklace.

(Approximate retail value $19.95)

Send for yours today...
compliments of 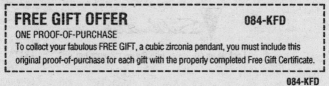 *Silhouette*®

To receive your free gift, a cubic zirconia pendant, send us one original proof-of-purchase, photocopies not accepted, from the back of any Silhouette Romance™, Silhouette Desire®, Silhouette Special Edition®, Silhouette Intimate Moments® or Silhouette Yours Truly™ title available in February, March and April at your favorite retail outlet, together with the Free Gift Certificate, plus a check or money order for $1.65 u.s./$2.15 can. (do not send cash) to cover postage and handling, payable to Silhouette Free Gift Offer. We will send you the specified gift. Allow 6 to 8 weeks for delivery. Offer good until April 30, 1997 or while quantities last. Offer valid in the U.S. and Canada only.

Free Gift Certificate

Name: _____

Address: _____

City: _____ State/Province: _____ Zip/Postal Code: _____

Mail this certificate, one proof-of-purchase and a check or money order for postage and handling to: SILHOUETTE FREE GIFT OFFER 1997. In the U.S.: 3010 Walden Avenue, P.O. Box 9077, Buffalo NY 14269-9077. In Canada: P.O. Box 613, Fort Erie, Ontario L2Z 5X3.

FREE GIFT OFFER   084-KFD
ONE PROOF-OF-PURCHASE
To collect your fabulous FREE GIFT, a cubic zirconia pendant, you must include this original proof-of-purchase for each gift with the properly completed Free Gift Certificate.

084-KFD

And the Winner Is...
You!

...when you pick up these great titles
from our new promotion at your
favorite retail outlet this June!

Diana Palmer
The Case of the Mesmerizing Boss

Betty Neels
The Convenient Wife

Annette Broadrick
Irresistible

Emma Darcy
A Wedding to Remember

Rachel Lee
Lost Warriors

Marie Ferrarella
Father Goose

New York Times Bestselling Authors

JENNIFER BLAKE
JANET DAILEY
ELIZABETH GAGE

Three *New York Times* bestselling authors bring you three very sensuous, contemporary love stories—all centered around one magical night!

It is a warm, spring night and masquerading as legendary lovers, the elite of New Orleans society have come to celebrate the twenty-fifth anniversary of the Duchaise masquerade ball. But amidst the beauty, music and revelry, some of the world's most legendary lovers are in trouble....

Come midnight at this year's Duchaise ball, passion and scandal will be...

Unmasked

Revealed at your favorite retail outlet in July 1997.

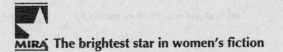

MIRA The brightest star in women's fiction

MANTHOL

twins
on the doorstep
by Stella Bagwell

When the Murdock sisters found abandoned twins
on their ranch-house doorstep, they had no clue the
little ones would lead them to love!

Come see how each sister meets her match—and how
the twins' family is discovered—in

THE SHERIFF'S SON (SR #1218, April 1997)

THE RANCHER'S BRIDE (SR #1224, May 1997)

THE TYCOON'S TOTS (SR #1228, June 1997)

TWINS ON THE DOORSTEP—a brand-new miniseries
by Stella Bagwell starting in April...
Only from

Silhouette ROMANCE™

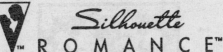

COMING NEXT MONTH

It's a month of your favorite wedding themes! Don't miss:

#1234 AND BABY MAKES SIX—Pamela Dalton

Fabulous Fathers/It's A Girl!

Single father Devlin Hamilton agreed to a *platonic* marriage with lovely Abby O'Reilly. Their children needed a real family—and Devlin and Abby could help each other without the added risk of true love. Until a surprisingly passionate wedding night led to a new family addition!

#1235 THREE KIDS AND A COWBOY—Natalie Patrick

Second Chance At Marriage

Playing the part of the loving wife wasn't difficult for Miranda Sykes. She still loved her soon-to-be ex-husband, and Brodie needed her to adopt the orphans he'd taken in. But Miranda hadn't realized that three kids and a cowboy just might change her mind about staying around forever!

#1236 JUST SAY I DO—Lauryn Chandler

Substitute Groom

A fake engagement to dashing Adam Garrett would finally rid once-jilted bride Annabelle of everyone's pity. But when sparks started to fly between her and her substitute groom, their arrangement didn't feel like a game anymore! Could Annabelle get Adam to just say "I do" for real?

#1237 THE BEWILDERED WIFE—Vivian Leiber

The Bride Has Amnesia!

Dean Radcliffe's nanny had lost her memory…and thought she was Dean's wife and mother of his children! Until Susan remembered the truth, the handsome single father had to play along, but could it be this bewildered woman was meant to *truly* be his wife?

#1238 HAVE HONEYMOON, NEED HUSBAND—Robin Wells

Runaway Bride

After jilting her two-timing fiancé, Josie Randall decided to go on her dude ranch honeymoon—alone. Falling for wrangler Luke O'Dell was the last thing she'd expected—but the brooding, stubborn rancher soon lassoed her love, and had her hoping this honeymoon could land Luke as a husband!

#1239 A GROOM FOR MAGGIE—Elizabeth Harbison

Green Card Marriage

A marriage of convenience to her arrogant boss was drastic, but Maggie Weller would do anything to stay with Alex Harrison—and care for his adorable little girl. But Maggie's green-card wedding led not only to a permanent position in Alex's home, but to a most *unexpected* place in his heart!